W9-AAX-892

THE
CHAMBER
IN THE SKY

THE CHAMBER IN THE SKY

THE NORUMBEGAN QUARTET VOLUME 4

M. T. ANDERSON

SCHOLASTIC PRESS
NEW YORK

Copyright © 2012 by M. T. Anderson

Library of Congress Cataloging-in-Publication Data Available

ISBN 978-0-545-33493-8

10 9 8 7 6 5 4 3 2 1
12 13 14 15 16

Printed in the U.S.A.   23
First edition, June 2012

The text was set in 11-pt. Excelsior.
Book design by Steve Scott

To N, D, and T
in the House of Hounds

PROLOGUE

Mr. and Mrs. Thatz stood in a motel room in Gerenford, Vermont, staring at the air conditioner. They were waiting for a call from the police. Their son, Brian, and his friend Gregory had been missing for days. At this point, the police thought it was unlikely that the boys were still alive.

"They're gone," whispered Mrs. Thatz. "Don't tell me they're not." She stood in front of the air conditioner. It jumbled her hair.

"We don't know they're gone," said her husband. "Things, you know, show up. People show up."

"They're gone, Steve."

"Don't say that."

"They're gone." She started to cry.

The boys had disappeared without a trace. A week ago, they'd taken a train to spend a weekend in the mountains with Gregory's cousin Prudence. They were supposed to have called each day they were there. But they hadn't.

Instead Prudence had called and left a message that no one could understand.

When the Thatzes had discovered their son had vanished, they'd taken the first train to Vermont. They had seen the house where Prudence lived and where the boys had slept at least one night. The windows were smashed and the door hung open. It looked like there had been a riot. There were planks nailed to the window frames and black streaks burned onto one of the walls.

Now the Thatzes stood in their Vermont motel room and waited for someone to call. Mr. Thatz flipped his phone open. "I'm going to listen to the message again."

"Okay," said Mrs. Thatz. She turned away.

Mr. Thatz hit 1 to play his messages. The first and only one saved was from Prudence, left a few days before. She had called both the Stoffles and the Thatzes, one after the other, from a pay phone in the local Halt'n'Buy. The message made no sense to them.

"Hi, it's Prudence. Mr. and Mrs. Thatz? Hi ... Look, Gregory and Brian — I can't explain, but they're ... they're okay. ... Not really. They're not okay. They've gone away, but they're coming back. I'm going to make sure. Don't worry. Look, there are these ... there are people called the Thusser. ... They're coming. Brian and Gregory are trying to stop them. I know that sounds — All right. I'm sorry. I don't know how to explain anything. I've got to get back under the mountain. I have to be there when they try to come back. But I just wanted you to know that — don't worry. Or ... I don't know. Maybe

2

worry." Then, very rushed, *"Look. Bye. I'll tell you . . . soon. Bye."*

Mr. Thatz stood with the phone to his ear after the message played. A metallic woman's voice asked him whether he would like to delete the message, play it again, call back, or save it. He murmured, "Save it." He didn't move except to break the connection with a nudge of his thumb. He still faced out the window.

" 'People called the Thusser,' " Mrs. Thatz repeated. She stared at the bed.

Mr. Thatz asked, "What does she mean?"

"Who knows?" said Mrs. Thatz. She shook her head with disapproval. "That girl."

Mr. Thatz closed the phone. He handed it to one of the men in long overcoats who sat on the bed. Their eyes were entirely black — no white, no iris. Their ears were long and pointed. There were three of them sitting on the bed.

"Honey," Mr. Thatz said, "I was thinking of going out to get some subs. Want one?"

"I'm not hungry," said Mrs. Thatz.

The men watched them from the bed and from the chair, and one was curled up on the floor, chewing away at something he'd found in the knocked-over trash can.

Mr. Thatz stared out the window. In the parking lot, Thusser men and women with black-orbed eyes stood around in groups of two or three. A car was overturned on the bright green lawn. A line of human children in summer shorts and grubby tees walked past as if in a

3

dream. A man had collapsed on the balcony and lay facedown.

A platoon of Thusser soldiers marched by on their way to another town, another church steeple, another mini-mall. No one seemed to notice them.

Down in the motel office, the desk clerk had almost been absorbed by the desk, though much of his head, one of his eyes, and all of his hair could still be seen. The gray surface of the desktop was pocked and bubbled with acne where it met and submerged his cheek. His fingers, projecting from the desk like a corpse's from ice, twitched around the key to room 27.

Shut up in the closet, his girlfriend lurked and hissed like a cat.

ONE

In another world lay the Great Body. No one knew what it looked like on the outside — whether it had flippers or feet or limbs at all. Its alien organs sprawled across unimaginable distances, crammed into arches of skeleton more massive than mountains. Entrails were wound around systems of stomachs as large as continents. And deep in one of those stomachs, Thusser soldiers spread like an infection — tiny, black-clad figures skating across great flat marshes of slime to invade the higher organs.

Elsewhere, hanging from spurs of bone, there were clusters of hearts, each brimming with a different liquid — some a glaring blue, others cool and green.

In one heart, there was no blood. The valves that might have once pumped some foreign fluid were stopped up, crammed with a tangled growth of fibers. In the two huge chambers of that Dry Heart was a desert, lined with crystal salts.

Far off in that shining desert, slowly approaching the forest of fibers at the tip of the ventricle, leaving tracks that stretched almost back to the ramshackle city of New Norumbega, was a small company of kids on beasts.

Their lumbering steeds each had seven limbs and no head. The beasts were called thombulants; they were painted with stripes and curlicues of crumbling pigment. The riders were teens. One was a girl with fine, aristocratic features, dressed in riding clothes: jodhpurs and a bright red jacket. One was a blond, slim boy with a sly, sarcastic grin. And following their steeds by a few monstrous paces was a thickset boy with black hair and greasy glasses, sweating in the light cast by glowing arteries far above.

The two in front were discussing their favorite smells.

"No way!" said the blond boy, Gregory Stoffle, slapping his saddle. "I love new paint, too!"

"And jasmine," said the girl, whose name was Gwynyfer Gwarnmore and who would some day be Duchess of the Globular Colon.

Brian Thatz rode behind them sullenly. He took off his glasses and rubbed them on his shirt. He couldn't get the lenses clean anymore. He was afraid they'd been scratched, somewhere between him crawling through caverns under Mount Norumbega, scampering through a war-torn shanty city under assault by a race of mechanical servants, and ducking from the detonation of a do-it-yourself elfin palace blown to bits by its explosive overlord.

"Fritos," declared Gregory, "sometimes smell like the best kind of grease in the world, and sometimes just smell like toes. Mystery."

Gwynyfer Gwarnmore laughed. She fixed her long, rippling hair beneath its black riding cap. She was about to name another thing that smelled good when Brian interrupted.

He said, "We're almost at the Wildwood." He pointed ahead. About half a mile on, the huge gray strands and fibers were raveled in massive loops and knots. The walls of the heart were clearly tapering now, and all the little veins and arteries could be seen, scribbled on the sky. "Is there anything we should know?"

Gwynyfer glanced back at him. "You don't spare a great deal of time for chuckles, do you, Brian? You're very tense-making."

"I just want to get to Archbishop Darlmore, find out about the way to get the Rules Keepers to return, and prevent the Thusser from invading. I just . . ." He stopped miserably.

"No favorite smells?" Gwynyfer asked.

Brian frowned. He looked toward the tangles of weird growth sprouting in the tip of the heart. The three beasts and their riders trudged on.

They were on their way into the Wildwood, which clogged the tips of the Dry Heart. Many years before, Archbishop Darlmore, brother of the Empress of these infinite Innards, had given up life in the Court of New Norumbega and had tramped off into the wilderness to become a hermit. He was tired of the elfin Court and its

7

frivolity. He was exasperated by their games and their tea dances, their boredom and their cruelty.

Unfortunately, he was the only courtier who had paid attention to the Norumbegans' treaty with the Thusser, their great rival among the sublime races. He was the only one who knew how to stop the Thusser from expanding to take over all of New England, upon the Earth, and all of the digestive, pulmonary, and cardiac tracts in the Great Body. If the kids couldn't find him, there was no way they could stand up against the brilliant sorcery and wicked cunning of the Thusser, who they knew were creeping up from the stomachs toward the Dry Heart itself.

Brian felt a constant anxiety about how far the Thusser had extended their dominion upon the Earth. He knew that time moved differently back there, and that the Thusser had been invading the dreams and the lawns of Vermonters for months now. For all Brian and Gregory knew, each minute spent giggling about snack chips and foot stench was a whole day back on Earth, flipping between dark and light, with neighborhoods falling and humans trapped within their own homes like cattle while the Thusser milked their minds.

Years ago, when Brian had been just a little kid, he had read books of British fairy tales, and they always said that the elves were not like humans, that they didn't understand the importance of things the same way, that the idea of "right" and "wrong" confused them, and that they kept to strange rules. Brian hadn't realized what that meant until he met Norumbegans like Gwynyfer.

For the last few days, she had been constantly cheerful, but it seemed like nothing mattered to her like it should. She didn't seem particularly worried about the approach of the murderous Thusser through the stomach of Three-Gut. She certainly didn't care that hundreds of humans had already vanished back on Earth. But the previous night when they camped, she'd almost been in tears when she saw the wrinkles in her tweed riding costume. ("*Nothing* ever stays perfect! Nothing in this world or the others!")

She was, at least, not being as mean to Brian as she had been a few days before. Now she treated him like a little brother. She was always giggling at him for being dull, but the jokes were gentle and even affectionate. She thought he had saved her and her family from an accusation of murder.

When he thought about this, Brian couldn't even look in her direction — at her slim back swaying on the rippling, ponderous thombulant. Because he had not just saved her and her family from that accusation — he had also, without her knowledge, been the person who had accused her in the first place. It was awful to think about. He'd almost made a terrible mistake.

She didn't know any of this. But Gregory did, and Gregory was still angry about it. Gregory still glared sometimes at Brian, or hinted that Brian should be more friendly as they traipsed across the burning desert of the Dry Heart.

Brian just wanted it all to be over. He wished he and his best friend could just leave the Great Body and never

9

come back. He wanted to be home. But instead, he was confronted by the tangled Wildwood. They could now see where some of the fibers grew out of the walls and the desert floor itself. It was unclear whether the tendrils were some kind of parasite, rooted in the salty plain, or whether they were part of the alien heart itself.

Brian said, "My mom's spaghetti sauce."

"What?" said Gregory.

"My favorite smell," explained Brian glumly. "She uses white wine and some cinnamon. She makes it once a week."

His friend shot him a look of annoyance. "Great," said Gregory. "Fascinating." He asked Gwynyfer, "So, how do we find Archbishop Darlmore in that big mess?"

"He's no longer an archbishop. After he went flitters and became a hermit, he was defrocked."

"Undressed?"

"No. Just had the pointy hat taken away. And some absolutely darling brocade skirts." She half turned in her saddle and rummaged in one of her saddlebags, pulling out a map drawn with ballpoint pen on the back of an envelope. "The Empress's directions aren't *absolutely* clear. There are roads bored through the Wildwood. We follow the main one in and then we go . . . why, I guess sort of wiggly to the left." She turned the envelope sideways and traced the route again. "It should be obvious when we get there."

They entered the Wildwood. Great cables uncoiled around them. Each one was ten or twenty feet across, at least. The mess loomed above them, a vast gray cloud of looped confusion.

The road was a set of five thick strands braided together. It rose above the heart's floor and led directly into the tangle. The kids and their thombulants continued without a word.

It took some time before Gregory and Gwynyfer began whispering cutely to each other again.

Around lunchtime, they reached a small village hanging from stalks. Gwynyfer suggested that they buy some meat pies at a store there and save their provisions for later.

"Great idea," said Gregory. He started to climb down the leather ladder from his saddle before he noticed that Gwynyfer wasn't moving. "You coming?" he asked.

She laughed. "Into the *bakery*? No. When one is of the blood of the ancient families of Norumbega, one doesn't speak to hawkers of meat pies. Or carry small change."

"So you're staying here."

She smiled. "Quite. Sitting haughtily astride my steed."

"And Brian and I are going in."

"Otherwise, they'd have to purify the room before I visited. In a ritual. It's kinder to them, really, if I stay outside. They'd be terribly put out." She made a cute little wave. "So . . . thanks much!"

Brian and Gregory went in to buy the pies.

As they climbed a winding staircase to the dangling bakery, Gregory looked back at her. She was poised on top of her thombulant, fastening the straps on her saddlebags.

"Doesn't she look amazing?" said Gregory. "Come on. She is a girl who looks great on a big, seven-legged monster. She sits the best on a seven-legged monster of any girlfriend I've ever had."

Brian didn't say anything.

"Don't get all sour," said Gregory. His eyes got hard. "Last week, you accused her of murder. And you were wrong."

Brian shrank. "I know," he said. "I feel really dumb."

"She thinks you're some big hero. She's being really nice to you. *Really* nice. So don't be such a jerk about her."

Brian nodded, accepting his scolding. He opened the door to the bakery.

When they came out with the pies, Gwynyfer couldn't believe they'd gotten her chicken. She wanted something called tongue of vunch. She sent Gregory back.

He bowed like a butler, smirked, and jogged back up the steps to get her everything she asked for.

She clapped with delight to see him run.

✳ ✳ ✳

That night, they slept at an inn that swung from several strands beside the braided road. Gregory and Gwynyfer sat for a long time on a balcony overlooking the whorl of fibers. The building rocked quietly as they sat whispering to each other about sports teams they

12

followed. The ice in their drinks rattled from side to side as the inn rocked. They held up their palms to stop their glasses from sliding off the overturned crate that served as a table.

Brian was trying to sleep in his room. He hated the motion of the inn. It made him slightly seasick. He could hear the other two talking on the balcony.

None of them noticed that another guest was slipping down the staircase, wearing complicated goggles. They did not see him creep out to the stable across a rope bridge. They didn't hear the creak of the stable's side door, or see him disappear inside.

Ten minutes later, he was climbing the stairs again, his odd, inhumanly bunched body hopping giddily with each step.

✳ ✳ ✳

In another day, the three had turned off the main road and were deep into the tangle. They no longer passed shacks hanging from the strands above them like hard-scrabble Christmas ornaments. They rode single file on a couple of strands that were bound every once in a while with a loop of fiber.

They came across a notice board sticking out of the path at a crossroads. There was mail tacked to it, and a couple of copies of the *Norumbega Vassal-Tribune* were nailed open so people passing could read the stories of the week. Brian saw the headlines, which were disastrous

13

and all too familiar: The invading Thusser Horde had taken over the mannequin fortress of Pflundt, and now controlled all of Three-Gut; the palace at New Norumbega had exploded; there was a new truce with the Mannequin Resistance, who were aiding in the defense against the Thusser; there was a benefit concert to aid the nobles who'd lost their mansions in the recent fighting: the New Norumbegan Consort would be playing a program of composer Gwion Bach's symphonies for lutes, harps, violins, and viols made of various skulls (wolf, cow, and griffon).

As Brian read the news, the path jounced once. He didn't take much notice of it.

"Notice boards like this are how the country people get their messages," Gwynyfer explained. "It's rather charming and rustic." She pointed through the tangle. "And there's an old family cemetery."

Far off were suspended the corpses of dead elves. They had been baked into shells of dough. Spells or prayers were written on their bodies in icing. They had hung there for years and the dough was cracked. Shoulders and legs of blackened, mummified bodies showed through.

"It's sweet," said Gwynyfer. "You don't normally see a graveyard like that anymore."

The road shuddered again. Brian looked along its length. Other strands around them were quivering. He didn't like it. He clutched the reins of his beast.

"We turn here," said Gwynyfer, checking her map. "That way."

Gregory shouted a warning.

Brian turned and looked.

14

Some vast, gigantic mite was descending from a drooping cable above them. Its legs were many, jagged and jointed as lightning. Each ended in a needle it plunged into the fronds of the Wildwood to hold itself up. It hurtled toward the three kids and their steeds.

Brian fumbled with his saddlebags, reaching for his Norumbegan musket, which hung from two straps. He twisted around in the saddle, furiously working at the buckles.

"Come on!" Gregory shouted to his own beast, whacking his heels into its sides. "Run! Run, you idiot!" Gregory took his goad and walloped it. The steed picked up a gentle canter. Gregory jolted along in the saddle, hollering, "No, *run!*"

Then Gregory's great, seven-legged thombulant stopped in its tracks. Gregory's shoulders snapped forward. He almost fell off. The thombulant stumbled, then jumped, as if it had kicked up its back legs.

Gregory looked back.

His steed hadn't jumped; one of the giant mite's needle-sharp feet had plunged into the thombulant's back. A muddy, blue line shot up the jointed leg toward the monster — the thombulant's blood. The mite was sucking the life out of the poor beast.

Gregory screamed. The mite was dragging him and his collapsing steed closer to the edge of the path.

The boy scrambled to hold on to the pommel of his saddle. He felt his steed, dying of blood loss, lifted in the air.

With a final yelp — strangely quiet and short — he fell.

15

TWO

Brian saw Gregory's dead thombulant drop off the cable and rebound on loops and arcs far below, dwindling. He saw also that Gregory had fallen out of the saddle first — luckily — and had dropped onto the path. The blond boy lay on his back, stunned, his arms twitching, his mouth open, the wind knocked out of him.

By now, Brian had his musket out. He pointed it at the monster's body and gathered his thoughts together to say the Cantrip of Activation — the magical trigger word that would fire the gun.

But it was hard to think with his steed bucking beneath him, panicked, releasing steam from fluttering vents.

The giant mite did not seem interested in him. It now moved with mechanical swiftness toward Gwynyfer and her frantic thomb.

Brian barked the Cantrip of Activation, and the gun fired.

16

He saw a blast of light spray across the monster's thick, lumpy hide. He'd hit it square in the middle of its huge, hulking body.

But it made no difference. The skin was too thick.

The monster fastened itself to the nearest strands for purchase and darted two legs toward Gwynyfer's riding beast. She screeched at it and swung her goad, knocking one of the needle-like arms back.

Brian fired again.

And once again, it didn't make any difference whatsoever.

The monster shot its jointed arms out once more and this time pierced the flesh of Gwynyfer's steed with two of its syringe claws. It began to suck blood. The blue line of liquid shot up its arms.

Another brown, needled arm slashed down — and this time, it shot right at Gwynyfer, tearing her red riding coat. Then it reared back and prepared to shoot forward one last time.

Brian was in a panic. His gun was useless, Gregory was lying helplessly on the ground, unable to speak — and now Gwynyfer was about to be drained of her blood.

Then he had an idea. He aimed again, only this time higher. He thought of the Cantrip of Activation and fired.

One of the giant mite's thin, zigzag legs blasted apart at a joint. The monster quivered.

Brian fired again and again at the legs that held the thing suspended in air.

The monster swayed crazily now, trying to retract its syringe legs from its prey to fasten them on another strand.

17

Brian blew another leg off.

The mite was running out of legs to hold itself up.

Gwynyfer, once more in a perfect riding pose, shouted to her thombulant, "Go on, then!" Her steed charged forward, freeing itself from the needles.

Brian blasted apart another leg — and at this, the giant mite slewed to the side, tried to plunge a remaining needle into a stalk — failed — and fell.

It slapped briefly against the path, and the path shuddered a little. The monster kept falling.

They heard the metallic reports of the thing banging against fibers below.

Brian took a deep breath. He rode his steed over to the edge of the path and looked down. The shadowy tangle still wobbled where the monster had fallen.

Gregory was standing up, looking pale and shaken. Gwynyfer reined in her steed. "Lovely, Bri-Bri!" she exclaimed. She did not seem shaken in the least. "Gregory, you poor thing. Look at you, all dismounted."

Gregory couldn't speak immediately. He kept looking around, fixing his eyes on the quivering fibers.

"I can't believe I didn't fall off the path," he said, stunned. "It was a mistake. I didn't mean to get out of the saddle. I was trying to stay on, but then it, uh . . ."

"Well, bravo to you for your lack of skill and coordination." Gwynyfer tapped her goad playfully against the hide of her recovering steed. "You know what's just the biggest crying shame? That you'll have to walk from now on. Walking's bad for the knees."

18

Gregory looked at her in bewilderment. Then he realized that she was flirting, and started to smile. "Unless I could catch a ride from some lovely lady."

"Losers, weepers."

Regardless, Gregory started to clamber up the side of her steed.

She urged it to skip forward. It took a quick step. Gregory fell, hitting the path hard.

"Uff!" he exclaimed. He looked up at her in surprise.

She said, "I fancy more back-and-forth between us. More 'Please, Gwynyfer, please, ha-ha-ha.' And us smiling darlingly at each other and the musical ringing of my clear, bell-like laugh rippling through the aorta."

"Sorry," said Gregory. "I forgot about the musical ringing of your clear, bell-like laugh."

"Rippling. So you did."

Brian waited.

He still held the musket. He watched for the mite to return from below.

✳   ✳   ✳

That particular mite did not return. The next day, they saw another one far above them, and it began to scuttle down, but Brian was ready this time, and just a few warning shots frightened it off.

They were deep, deep in the Wildwood. They were no longer on a path made of even a couple of strands tied together. They now tramped along a single strand. It

19

bobbed continually. Brian hated the motion. He gripped his reins and his goad tightly.

Gregory rode behind Gwynyfer. They kept poking each other and laughing. Brian couldn't hear much of what they said. It was mainly about her childhood in the Globular Colon.

Shortly before noon, they came to the far side of the Wildwood. They saw the wall of the Dry Heart, bristling with the bases of fronds as thick as skyscrapers.

There among the trunks hung a hut. It had many roofs, all of them shingled, and several bridges that led to out-buildings hanging on the pinky-gray flesh of the wall. A few of the smaller fronds — still large as tree trunks — grew right through the hut, curling out of holes in the walls. None of the windows matched.

"There it is," said Gwynyfer as they approached. "At least according to the Empress. Her brother's hermit hut." A final time, she checked the envelope with the directions on it. Then she lightly tossed it away. Brian watched it waft over the side of the path and flutter downward, rocking back and forth on breezes.

He hoped that throwing it out hadn't been a mistake.

As they got closer to the hut, they heard something creaking. The sound was lazy and rhythmic. Brian gently pulled the reins toward him. His thombulant slowed.

A man rocked in a chair on the front porch. He sat quietly, watching them. Around him were things that might have been giant slugs or chickens — balls of feather with long, wet necks or tails sticking out of each end. Several of them hung from the woodwork on the porch, sleeping.

The man did not move while he watched the kids approach, even when they held up their hands to greet him.

In human terms, the archbishop Thomas Darlmore looked to be about sixty-five. He was handsome and tired and severe. His head was as gaunt as a thermos. His cheeks had deep channels in them. His hair was buzz cut and stuck straight up, gray and metallic. He wore a cable-knit fisherman's sweater and khakis that were splattered with paint. He had a book in one hand.

The chicken lumps played at his feet.

Gwynyfer called up to him, "The Honorable Gwynyfer Gwarnmore, daughter of His Grace Cheveral Gwarnmore, Duke of the Globular Colon, greets the Most Reverend and Right Honorable Thomas Darlmore, Archbishop of Norumbega, and requests audience and asylum, bearing greetings from his fond and devoted sister, the Empress of the Innards."

Brian waited anxiously for the old man to reply. The formal language of the Imperial Court made Brian jumpy. He couldn't understand half of it, even though it was magically translated.

The man stared down at them. Finally, he said, in a hoarse voice, "No archbishop here." He lifted a chicken thing off his shoe. "Defrocked."

Gwynyfer bowed her head, smiled radiantly at him, and began again. "The Honorable Gwynyfer Gwarnmore, daughter of His Grace Cheveral Gwarnmore, Duke of the Globular Colon, greets Mr. Thomas Darlmore, beloved brother of our Sublime Highness Elspeth Fendritch, Empress of the Innards, and regrets that so many are

Mr. Darlmore's glories that Miss Gwarnmore does not know by which title to address him, any more than she might choose one beam of the sun's radiance above the rest that fall so plenteously upon the —"

"Honey," grated the man in the rocking chair, "you've never seen the sun once. And I'll never see it again." He sighed and closed his book, leaving his finger in the page. "Listen, kids, we're way down at the plug-end of the heart here. Nothing to do but fly-fish in the bloodstream. I haven't worn socks in seventy-three years. So forget 'Your Radiant Lordship.' Drop the verbs in the sixth-person-disembodied formal. Clear?"

Gwynyfer was clearly unhappy about being interrupted. She said, "If Mr. Darlmore will be so good as to indicate which title best suits him, he will cease to discompose his devoted supplicant."

The ex-archbishop said, "I'm Tom. You're Gwyn. And they're human?" He pointed vaguely at Brian and Gregory.

"You got it, sir," said Gregory cheerfully. "Brian Thatz over there, and I'm Gregory Stoffle."

Thomas Darlmore nodded. He got up and laid his book on the railing. He looked askance at its cloth cover a while, then he called down, "You say my sister's Empress?"

Gwynyfer confirmed it.

Darlmore nodded, thinking this over. "What about Rands?" he asked. "He dead?"

Gwynyfer said, "With delight, Miss Gwarnmore reports that Randall Fendritch, beloved husband of the Empress, is alive and flourishes."

"And my nephew? Last I heard, they'd made him Emperor so Elspeth and Rands could go off, improve their golf swings."

The kids didn't really know how to answer this one politely. They each waited for someone else to say something until Gregory finally blurted out, "Your nephew exploded. It turned out he was a bomb."

Thomas Darlmore heard this and threw up his hands, as if to say, *Of course, of course.* He squinted down at the kids. "Some Thusser doctor involved? Something similar, once before, back in the reign of Nimrod. Some Thusser shamans got their hands on the Empress. All the heirs were spirals or piles of dust. A fistful of glass rods."

"We're sorry about your nephew, Mr. Darlmore," said Brian.

Darlmore didn't answer. For a long time, he stared off into the Wildwood.

Looking carefully at the ex-archbishop, Brian suddenly caught a glimpse in him of the young man they'd seen a year before in visions and time-slips back in Old Norumbega. They'd seen him dashing through the forest, hunting with the Emperor and Empress. They'd seen him sitting on a pleasure barge on a black, underground lake with all the Court around him, watching an aquatic ballet. They'd seen him dressed in silk brocade robes and a pointed hat sewn with cloth of gold.

And now he stood in his paint-splattered pants, staring out into a jungle of growths that stoppered up a big, dead heart.

Brian said, "Sir, we're . . . we're very glad to meet you. We've come a long way to talk to you."

Darlmore looked at the boy but didn't speak.

Brian continued. "We, um, we heard you left the Court because they wouldn't take anything seriously. Like the Thusser Hordes. Well, we're here because the Hordes have broken the rules of the Game and have taken over Old Norumbega and they're . . ."

Darlmore waited, but Brian was too nervous to continue. The man's stare was hard and blue and intense.

The hermit shooed chicken slugs away from a trapdoor, opened it, and dropped a rope ladder through. He clambered down to help the kids dismount.

"You'll want to park your thombs." He gestured with his head over toward an outbuilding that was strapped to the strand. "There's feed in there. You should —" He sniffed. He walked closer to Gwynyfer's thombulant and drew in a series of sharp breaths.

Gwynyfer was clearly repelled by the hermit sniffing her steed.

Darlmore asked, "What's this? Doesn't smell like thombs."

"You mean Brian?" said Gregory. "Oh, sometimes we give him breath mints. But no dice."

Darlmore shot Gregory an irritable look. "Your steed, Gwyn," he said.

"The Honorable Gwynyfer Gwarn —"

"You have something on your steed. It's been painted with something."

Gregory said, "I don't smell anything weird."

24

"How well do you know the smell of thombulants?" The hermit made his way along the flank of the beast, placing his hands on its hide, leaning close to it, taking in its awful scent. "It's been painted with an attractor. You get attacked by anything on the way here? Cardiac mites or anything?"

"Yeah!" said Gregory. "One almost killed me!"

Gwynyfer said graciously, "Bri-Bri there was the hero of the hour. He offed it."

Darlmore sniffed the other thombulant. "See, completely different. This one hasn't been painted."

"Huh?" said Gregory. "Been painted how?"

Darlmore asked him, "Were you riding one of these things, too?"

"Yeah."

"Yours was probably slathered up with attractor, too."

Gwynyfer asked, "What is sir talking about?"

"Where'd you stay last night?"

"We camped," said Brian. "Right on one of the strands."

"Night before?"

"An inn," said Gregory.

"You watch your beasts all night?"

"Of course not," said Gwynyfer. "The stableboy did."

"The stableboy didn't," said Darlmore.

"The stableboy should have."

Brian pressed him, "What do you mean? What's an attractor?"

The hermit said, "I mean: Someone tried to kill you."

THREE

The hermit made them a kind of lifeless pancake — one huge, flat, pasty flapjack in a frying pan as big as a wagon wheel. Apparently, he ate simply.

"Later, we'll fish for dinner," he said. He jerked a few chains to adjust the height of the frying pan over the fire in the center of the room.

He looked at the kids. "So who'd want to kill you?" He squinted at each one of them in turn, then asked Gwynyfer, "Anyone with a gripe against your father? I knew him, by the way. Is there anyone who'd inherit your title? If you died?"

Gregory said, "Whoa, whoa! So tell us what you're thinking."

Darlmore explained, "Someone sabotaged your caravan. Someone painted your thombs with an attractor — the juice they use out here to draw the mites when they're hunting them. In the Wildwood, people hunt the mites for food. Mites love the smell of the attractor juice. They scuttle down out of their nests and try to grab whatever's painted with it. Then, normally, the hunt closes in." He yanked a chain and the black pan slammed upward. The pancake whirled up floppily toward the chimney-hole, flipped, and slapped back down. Darlmore turned to the kids again. "But in your case, someone was trying to get the mites to come kill you."

Brian thought carefully, then wondered aloud, "So you think they were only trying to get Gwynyfer?"

"And probably your pal Greg here. Place bets they buttered up his thomb, too."

Gwynyfer patted Brian's hand and said sweetly, "It must be nice for once not to be the one people are trying to kill."

They ate the pancake. It was tough and dry.

"Sorry," said the hermit. "The lunch." He looked at Gwynyfer. "You want a napkin to spit it into?"

Gwynyfer replied haughtily, "The Honorable Miss Gwynyfer Gwarnmore has already used the tablecloth."

Brian said, "Sir, you're the only one at Court who used to worry about the Game, when you all were playing against the Thusser to see who'd rule Old Norumbega, back on our world."

Thomas Darlmore nodded.

Brian explained, "We're here because the Thusser have broken the rules. They're not playing the Game right anymore. They've invaded our world. They're settling all of New England. We can stop them, if someone here would just, you know, summon the Rules Keepers. The ones

27

who were supposed to make sure neither side cheated — the Norumbegans or the Thusser Horde. And Earth depends on it."

"Well, New England," Gregory corrected.

Darlmore walked over to the counter and got a pitcher of water. He refilled the kids' glasses. "One of the reasons I left the Court: I couldn't stand that they forgot the Game. We were better off in Old Norumbega. All this" — he put down the pitcher and gestured generally — "all the Great Body . . . it's a mistake to be here. It's too unstable. Might be dead. Might be dying. Might be alive and ready to convulse or stand up or sit down. We don't know." He turned away and began scraping the giant frying pan with a wooden spatula. "I used to believe we were going to win Old Norumbega back. I kept track of the Game . . . long time ago . . . long, long time . . . but the Court are all happy up there living in filth and smoking cheap cigarettes. I don't know, now." The spatula rasped on the black iron pan. "I don't know."

Irritably, Gwynyfer snapped, "They always speak very well of you, sir."

The hermit stopped scraping and stared at her. "Do they, Gwyn?" he said, and it was not a question. "Do they really?" He clearly knew the answer.

She flinched — then stared angrily right back at him.

Brian begged him, "But, Mr. Darlmore, you'll help us summon the Rules Keepers? The people at Court said that you're the only person who remembers how."

For a minute, the hermit didn't answer. He thwacked

the spatula against a coffee can to knock off burnt crisps. Then he said, "Sure."

Brian relaxed. He and Gregory grinned at each other.

Darlmore tossed the spatula into a tub of soap water. "The way to summon the Rules Keepers — it's a machine called the Umpire. Like a referee for the Game. It's a capsule. A little chamber. You go in it, there's a control set up by the Thusser and our Imperial Synod of Wizards. You activate it. It'll check the conduct of the Game and call the Rules Keepers." He went and leaned against a wide arch. "The capsule got washed away soon after the Court got here to the Great Body. Pretty soon after we first tried to settle here. You heard about the flooding? This mess came rushing down through the stomachs. Tragic. I'll tell you, almost everything was washed away. Whole carts of stuff. Mounds of furniture and so forth. People. Mannequins. The Umpire Capsule was lost, too."

"It's *gone*?" Brian exclaimed in despair.

Darlmore winced. "Not *gone*," he said. "I ran into it some years back. I was on an expedition. Wanted to see if there was a way out."

"A way out of what?" Gregory asked.

"The Great Body. I wanted to know whether there's an outside." He walked over, unrolled the tablecloth in front of Gwynyfer, removed the chunk of pancake she'd chewed, and then tossed it into the flame-pit in the center of the kitchen. "Theological question," he said.

Gregory said, "So was there?"

"A way out?"

"Yeah."

"I don't think there is," said the hermit. "I went right past the Globular Colon. Thought I might discover something. A passage to the exterior. See if there's skin. Limbs. A head. And others. Other Great Bodies floating through space. Or walking through an endless canyon." He shrugged. "Maybe there is a way out, but I didn't find it. Past the Globular Colon, there was just more gut. It's not like a human body or a Norumbegan body. The intestines split up and divide and go in different directions. They may not even be intestines. May not be for food. They get strange and corky."

"So where's the capsule, then?" Brian asked.

"I ran into it down in the guts. Joyful reunion, et cetera. It promised to write me sometimes. Pen pals."

"To *write* you?" said Gregory, astonished.

Gwynyfer said, "You didn't think it was important enough to bring it *back* with you? You didn't think of that?"

The hermit said harshly, "Quite. I didn't want the Court to get ahold of the thing."

"It belongs to the Emperor."

"Dear, you just told me the last Emperor exploded. It's safer for the Umpire down in the guts, moving around."

"How does it move around?" said Brian.

"On three mechanical giants. They carry it on their backs and they protect it. They keep it moving."

"It's *lost*!" Gwynyfer accused. "You *lost* it, sir!"

Darlmore strode under the arch and into a living room filled with big couches and chairs covered in batik cloths.

30

He slammed around at an old, broken desk and came back with a stack of postcards. "Not lost. The capsule sends me one of these occasionally." He tossed them down on the table.

Brian and Gregory leaned in to look at the stack of postcards. The photos showed odd buildings and weird, organic crevasses. There were cities of spikes. There were hotels on the shores of lakes of blue. There were plains filled with metal water tanks or oil tanks in rows. There were jungles of weird growth.

Darlmore flipped a few over to check the backs. He picked out one card. "Okay. See here."

On the front, the postcard had a picture of a tall, tall, thin stack of houses, steeples, and turrets in a rolling, green landscape. It said,

Greetings from the **JEJUNUM!**

"Wherever the heck the Jejunum is," said Gregory.

Gwynyfer explained, "There are four of them. They're way down in the Innards, at the entrance to the Volutes. They grow a lot of wheat there." She pushed back her hair with one hand. "You have to travel through one of them to get to the Globular Colon. It's pretty."

Darlmore had flipped the postcard over. On the back was a message scrawled in brown ink in large, clumsy Norumbegan runes. It said:

SIR WE ARE TIRED OF WANDERING THE VOLUTES AND SO WE HAVE EMERGED AND NOW WE STOP IN THE TOWN OF TURNSTILE AND REST. MAY JOY AND DELIGHT BE YOUR CONSTANT COMPANION YRS THE UMPIRE CAPSULE.

The postcard was from the Ellyllyn Inn, Turnstile.

Darlmore went into the other living room and came back with an elaborate, hand-painted map. Organs and ducts stretched in every direction. "The town of Turnstile's here," he said, tracing the coil of an intestine and tapping. "The intestines of the Great Body aren't like human or Norumbegan entrails. They branch more and they lead to one another and there are many separate tracts. It's lucky the capsule has stopped at Turnstile. Much easier to find it there."

While Gwynyfer was carefully inspecting the map, Darlmore inspected the two boys. "The Game: I'm assuming you were the human pawns?"

Gregory said, "Yeah."

Darlmore jerked his head and pointed, summoning them all to follow him.

He led them up a rickety staircase. There was a cramped little office full of stacks of paper and old books and a swivel chair. A window stolen from some other building was plastered into the wall, looking out at the Wildwood. Darlmore dug around in the piles. He set aside dull-looking philosophy books to reveal an old computer printer. The plastic was yellowed with time. A continuous spill of paper looped out of it, hanging down to the floor. Darlmore lifted up the last few sheets and tore them off at the perforations. He scanned them quickly. "Haven't looked at these messages for ages. Sent by . . . Wee Snig."

"We know him!" said Brian, excited. "He helped run the Game!"

"You have a friend," said Gwynyfer, "who goes by the first name of *Wee*? What a surprising set of acquaintances you keep."

The hermit tore off strips of snaff. "These updates were sent automatically both to this terminal and to the communications room at the palace in New Norumbega."

Brian and Gregory looked at each other. Brian said, "We never heard anything about a communications room at the palace."

Darlmore said, "No surprise. They probably don't remember it's there."

Brian nodded.

Darlmore looked up and down the sheets, scanning them. "I really should have kept up with this. . . . Look, here. . . . . A little more than a year and a half ago, our time. Your time . . . how do you arrange your years?"

Brian looked where the hermit's thumb bit the paper. "That's last October! That's when we played our round of the Game!"

"I figured. The printer kept spitting things out."

Brian read Wee Snig's description of the Game they'd played the previous fall. It just said:

Oct. 12

Round 18 instituted.

2 hum. cubs (aet. 13/14) engaged via prev.
victor (P. Grendle).

Location: Mt. Norumbega and environs.

Magic within budget (as projected in
summation memo of 4/1). Other ont.
parameters as cited in ritual expenditure
memo of 7/6.

Oct. 21

Round 18 completed.

Winner: Norumbegan op.

Will commence work on Round 19 on 12/1.

TT anomalies to be discussed upon request
(minor; projected).

It was a lot less eventful than the real thing had been.
"What does it mean?" Brian asked.

34

Darlmore cleared his throat. "Two human cubs aged around thirteen or fourteen engaged as players... Norumbegan player won."

Brian and Gregory exchanged a glance. It was Brian who'd won, and Gregory was occasionally touchy about it.

"That's *it*?" said Brian. "That's all anyone ever learned about everything we did? All we went through?"

"No," said Darlmore. "No one at the palace even bothered to read this report. So they learned even less." He laid the papers back on the printer.

"What's the rest of that?" Brian asked.

"Let's go fishing," the hermit said.

✳   ✳   ✳

Darlmore led the three of them along a bridge that stuck out of the back of the house and plunged deep into the final tangle of growth that blocked the great valve of the Dry Heart.

Brian could not believe that Thomas Darlmore had given up and hadn't even bothered to check the news of the Game. Darlmore had left the Court because he was outraged, and now, here he was, as lazy as the rest of them. All of those terrifying hours they'd spent creeping through basements, solving riddles, splashing in freezing underground lakes, dodging throwing-stars, and fleeing scent-sensitive ogres — no one had been watching.

Darlmore made Brian almost mad.

It was not far until they reached a kind of boathouse half wedged into the fibers. Inside there was lots of tackle, nets, buoys, sinkers, anchors, and a table with a few candles almost burned down to nothing. The far wall was made of corrugated metal, and a door led through it.

The hermit rattled a key in the door and forced it open. Inside was a tiny space with lots of pleather cushions and bulby windows everywhere. The world outside those windows was black.

Darlmore took down two reels of fishing wire and knotted weird little lures to them. The lures glittered with plastic gems. He didn't talk, but whistled through his teeth.

He ushered the kids into the little dinghy and shut the door behind them. He locked it and shook it to make sure it was firm. He flicked a switch.

Outside the windows, electric lights went on.

They realized that they were in a small pod clamped to the side of the boathouse, which projected out into the stream of the flux — a green fluid that might have been the Great Body's blood. Now that the lights were on, they could see strange, fluttering growths drifting past.

With a tug on a rusty lever, Darlmore set them floating. He revved up a motor — which filled the pod with the smell of water and oil — and puttered out among the groping fronds into the deep green depths.

The reels of fishing line were snapped into slots. Darlmore showed them how to cast. They pressed a little spring-loaded trigger, and watched the line soar off into the drink. They reeled the line in with cranks.

Nothing that they saw looked vaguely like a fish. There were pulpy, tired things, and there were spiky, fast things. There were little golden, flashing things that were too small and fast to catch. They distantly glimpsed a few huge, blundering things that they were afraid would respond to the lights.

Surprisingly, they had a good time fishing. They called out to one another, and even Brian finally felt part of the action, clapping when Gregory caught something (which turned out to be some kind of bloodweed, but edible) and furiously reeling in a fish-thing of his own.

Gwynyfer had forgotten to dislike the ex-archbishop. She was chattering happily as she thumped a little air-lock drawer open to reveal her six-mouthed fish. "Won't this make a delightful supper? We once went fishing down in the Organelles, my mother and father and I. The catch was delish."

Darlmore clearly was pleased they'd enjoyed the little trip. He turned the boat around and headed back into the looming fronds. He steered them through grottos and around stems until they reached the boathouse. The dinghy attached to the wall with a magnetic *thump*.

They hadn't caught much, but they hoped it would be tasty. Gwynyfer even skipped sideways a few steps along the bridge back to the shack, pulling Gregory by the hand.

Darlmore threw open the door to the kitchen. "One minute. A fire," he said. "We'll get those stewing. Even the bloodweed."

Brian went upstairs to look at the Game printouts again. Gwynyfer and Gregory headed into the living room to sit in the hammocks that hung from the massive growth that ran up through the floor and out a hole in the wall

As Gregory swung Gwynyfer back and forth, she sang out, "I had a cousin or second cousin or something who had a tree growing through her living room. Like this. Third cousin, maybe? That branch of the family's very complicated."

"I have a cousin Prudence who I think you'd like. She's mastered wizardry and sarcasm."

"Impressive," said Gwynyfer, who didn't sound particularly happy to be compared with another woman, especially a human one.

Brian, meanwhile, stood alone, upstairs, scanning the other reports from Wee Sniggleping, the grumpy Norumbegan who'd helped to arrange the Game. The cramped study was getting dark.

The final few pages of the update were awful to read. Back when they'd been on Earth, Brian had seen the problems, the "anomalies," that the printouts described: The Thusser had built a settlement, altering time itself, subduing humans to act as anchors or mental food for the psychic hunger of their Horde. People were absorbed into their houses and became just another appliance. But all the changes happened gradually, thought quietly became difficult, and no one noticed until it was too late.

Brian hated to read the record of growing panic that Wee Snig had left. The first mention of trouble was from about four months before (as time had once run).

Apr. 15

Work on Round 19 proceeding.

Minor chronological anomaly detected in
roughly three square mile area.

May 7

Time-slip detected. Worried that it may be
related to time travel in Round 18? Please
advise.

May 25

Evidence that there may be Thusser
interference in time, geography. Please
contact for details.

June 2

Thusser op displacing time. Parameters
of displacement described below. Please
advise.

This one was followed by a lot of gibberish with numbers and letters that clearly had some technical meaning Brian couldn't understand.

June 7

Have not heard from Court re: Thusser op. Clear evidence of Thusser presence and movement.

Game violations likely: G34, C17, Pr7', Pr8, Pr9, others.

Date no longer applicable

Can no longer judge time interface. Irregular chronological movement. Please advise.

N/A

Major Thusser invasion under way. Please advise.

N/A

Bloody idiots I'm sitting here watching your
empire fall to bits will you please put down
your bloody lacrosse sticks long enough to
communicate

whole thing is going to hell

N/A

please help — please

wee s

N/A

please call

July 12

Anomaly explained. Pardon my confusion.
There was no Thusser incursion. The Thusser
were not involved. I am removing myself for
some time to Florida for a needed rest.

41

```
Florida is a flat, warm place where people
drive slowly. Thank you for your attention.


I am leaving.


Will re-initiate contact in some years.


Best,


Wee Snig
```

That was the last transmission received.

Brian could feel the rising panic in Snig's reports. No one had heard his pleas.

Brian thought of Wee Snig and Prudence, waiting for him on the other side of the dark gate between worlds. He hoped they were safe now.

He hoped everyone back in his world was safe.

And then he received a blow to the head.

Thwack!

He reeled — dropped, slammed against the desk.

He half turned.

Then he froze.

Something cold was held against his skull. A gun. And someone said, "Child, don't move. Death is much easier when it's fast."

FOUR

The hermit made dumplings. He scattered flour on the countertop. Behind him, the bloodweed and meat bobbed in the boiling stew.

As he cooked, Tom Darlmore frowned and wondered what to do. He'd spent a hundred years or more acting as the empire's last ward of the Umpire Capsule, the last courtier to pay attention to the Game. When he was off spelunking in the Volutes, looking for a way out of the Great Body, he'd heard rumors that the capsule still wandered, ready for activation. Farmers saw it stumping along mopily through forests of polyps. Shepherds talked of its mechanical giants lumbering out of the dark and sitting by campfires at night. Darlmore had spent two months tracing the rumors. He'd found the Umpire near South Worthington, just down the road a piece from the town of Mercer's 'testine. He'd considered whether to send it up toward the Dry Heart, but he'd decided against it. The idiots there would just fuss with the thing, break it, destroy it on purpose. There were dukes and duchesses who wanted to make sure that the Norumbegans never left the Great Body. Back on Earth, they'd been nothing; now they owned a whole kidney or a mine in the tripe. They'd built railroads, vineyards, plantations, castle keeps. They didn't want to lose what they'd gained.

Years. It had been years since he'd cared about the Game. He hadn't noticed when he'd given up. He'd just started to spend his time working on the cabin and nothing else. Repairing the shingles, or dragging great sheets of fiberskin up from the pit below to replace a wall that sagged. He built coops for the branfs, his sluglike feathered pets. The branfs laid eggs. The years went past. A couple times a month, he'd go in to Herm's Depot to sell branf and buy flour, and he'd pick up a postcard from the capsule. But he never wondered much, anymore, about whether he'd ever have to activate the thing and call the Rules Keepers. He just assumed that someday the Great Body would shift or swallow or stretch, and they'd all be engulfed in disaster. That would be it. The end. (He touched his forehead with a floury hand to stave off evil.)

And now these kids. These pawns. Here they were, filled with demands that something had to be done. He remembered when he'd believed that doing things was a good idea.

Maybe he'd go with them. Another voyage. Another adventure. Meet up with the capsule, press the buttons. Feel what it was like again to care about something.

With a new agitation in his fingers, he kneaded the dough.

Then he heard something. Someone was wailing.

Darlmore swiftly and softly walked out of the kitchen, out to the passageway where windows looked down at the path.

Down below: four little creatures milling around the kids' steeds. They were all ridges and blotches and fanned-out crests. Their legs were thin and tiger striped.

They were called imbraxls. They were used, he knew, to stalk prey in the Wildwood.

Two imbraxls sniffed at a steed. One slept. One was bored, and howled for its master.

Someone was here at the shack.

Darlmore stepped back.

Imbraxls would be able to follow attractor juice.

Whoever had crept around the kids' steeds at that inn hadn't necessarily wanted the three dead.

They'd wanted a scent to follow.

Someone had traced the kids here.

Darlmore straightened his back. He returned to the kitchen.

Through the arch, he whispered, "Greg. Gwyn. Brian. Here. Now. No questions."

But it was too late.

✳ ✳ ✳

The pistol knocked against Brian's skull.

"Where's the Umpire?" asked the gunman.

Brian protested, "I don't know!" — a little louder than he needed to. He hoped the others could hear that something was wrong.

45

The gunman's mouth was close to his ear. "Is the arch-bishop in the kitchen? Whipping up some dish?"

Brian knew the voice. It was Dr. Brundish, a spy for the Thusser who'd fled the palace in the midst of a siege.

Brian asked, "Why do you want him?"

"Where's the Umpire? Is it here in the hut? Does he have it here, child?"

"No it's *not*! It's not here!"

"Then where?"

"We don't know!"

"Quieter. Quieter."

"How'd you find us?" Brian asked. "How'd you know we were coming here?"

"You spoke many times of wanting to rouse the Rules Keepers. That is the old archbishop's odd hobby, see? I knew that he was somewhere in the Wildwood. So I waited at an inn on the only route into the forest until you arrived, so I could follow you by imbraxl and find him."

"You know, the stupid juice you painted on our thom-bulants almost got us killed. It attracted mites."

Brian felt the man shrug. "Thin you out," he said. "If I lost one precious child along the way . . . well, less of the brutal, brutal work of killing left for later."

At that, Brian flinched.

The doctor jammed the gun harder against his flesh. "Now. Where is the Umpire Capsule?"

"None of us know. What do you want it for?"

"Ready to fall down some stairs?"

A foot slammed into Brian's side and he was hurled

backward, tumbling toward the staircase. He grabbed at the wall, failed, watched his feet trip, but caught himself on the railing just in time. He spun. He was half sitting a few steps down. He crouched, unsure whether he should stand or duck.

Dr. Brundish wheezed and considered. "Interesting. I would have assumed you'd use your elbows more." Now Brian could see Brundish in full. The Thusser doctor stood above him, dressed in a long coat and dirty robes. His round glasses were pulled up on his pale forehead, and he no longer wore concealing makeup. There were dark rings around his eyes — the mark of the Thusser. His bulky, weird body shifted its mysterious lumps beneath his coat and tunic.

Dr. Brundish took a few steps closer to Brian and whispered, "Let's go meet the others. Will I have the pleasure of finding them with the capsule?"

Brian repeated, "We don't — know — where — it — is."

"There is an old tradition that a gentleman in your position should put your hands up."

Brian did. He walked down the stairs with the doctor right behind him.

In the kitchen, they found Gwynyfer and Gregory looking perplexed by the dumplings. Darlmore had just come in the back door from outside and was by the counter.

Everyone was shocked to see Brundish.

"My masters approach from the lower organs," the doctor said. "The tea dance is over."

Gwynyfer stepped proudly toward him and said, "The Honorable Miss Gwynyfer Gwarnmore, daughter of the Duke of the Globular Colon, demands —"

"Oh, clap a lock on it, Miss Gwarnmore. A month from now, His Grace your father will be lined up against a wall and shot with the rest of the yawning frat-lads of noble Norumbega. Burned in one big pile, they'll be." He clicked his tongue. "Down to a frazzle and black char."

Darlmore's face was as severe as a cliff. He pointed at the door. "Out," he said.

Dr. Brundish's mouth squirmed in his whiskers. "Archbishop? Yes?"

"Out."

"I'm looking for the Umpire Capsule. You have it?"

"I don't. Not here. It lives on its own."

"About where?"

"We don't know." He glowered at Brundish. "You the Imperial Surgeon?"

"Technically, chirurgeon." The doctor smiled and sucked his teeth. "Regrettably, I have abandoned my position."

"I hear my nephew exploded."

"Quite so. The young are full of such boundless energy."

"You built him as an implant and a bomb."

"Don't look at me, Archbishop. The youth was at an awkward age."

"You detonated the Emperor of the Innards."

"Not so, Archbishop. Not so. These bad lads stole away my three-way radio. I could detonate no one. It was the

48

Thusser Magister who hit the trigger. We're in the guts now, you know, the Thusser. The Horde works its way up toward the Dry Heart, even as we speak."

"What do you want with the Umpire?"

"You know exactly what I want with it, Archbishop. Now where do you have it tucked away?"

"I don't —"

"Tell me, Archbishop."

Darlmore shook his head. He said, "Defrocked."

"I recall. Where is it, sir? *Where?*"

Darlmore sneered at the doctor. All look of the hermit in his face dropped away, and he was once again a lord of the Norumbegan Court, brother of the Emperor, scoffing at the ancient enemy of his race.

Dr. Brundish snarled and fired his pistol.

There was a quick blip of light.

Darlmore's leg burst and he fell to the kitchen floor, spattered with his own blood.

Gregory stumbled back in shock, knocking into Gwynyfer. Even she looked frightened, her fairy features wide-eyed and alert.

Thomas Darlmore, once Archbishop of Norumbega, lay rocking in pain near the brick oven, gasping for breath. Blood soaked the leg of his khakis, spreading quickly across his knee.

Brundish reached out with his free hand and grabbed Brian by the hair, dragged the boy close to him, and stuffed the muzzle of his pistol into the boy's ear. "I'm no student of human anatomy," Dr. Brundish admitted to Darlmore. "The head. Important?"

Darlmore pulled himself up against the pie safe and scrabbled with his knee. "Stop," he said. "Stop."

Gregory and Gwynyfer looked wildly from one to the other.

Dr. Brundish sucked in breath through his teeth and blew it out in a whistle. "We need to know where the capsule is. So no one thinks any pretty, pretty thoughts about calling the Rules Keepers." He yanked on Brian's black hair. "Mr. Darlmore? One more chance."

Brian winced in pain. His hair was being torn out by its roots. The doctor continued, "How about we play the game this way? Whoever tells me where the capsule is gets to live. As a guarantee. Until I find the capsule. Then you may skip along." He smiled. His body shrugged its strange mass from side to side. "Anyone? I have plenty of bullets for you all. Who wishes to be the last to live?" He looked from face to face: Gwynyfer's, full of anger. Gregory's, gape-mouthed and confused. Brian's, pale and shivering. And finally, the ex-archbishop on the floor, who had collected himself and now seemed strong and even-tempered.

Thomas Darlmore spoke.

"Let's go," he said. "Come with me upstairs. I can tell you where the capsule's waiting."

50

FIVE

The lumpy doctor released his grip on Brian's scalp. Brian felt the oddly jointed fingers slip out of his hair. He backed away as Brundish skittered a couple hops to the side.

The boy breathed deeply and held himself up against a counter. His ear still hurt from where the gun had been jammed into it. He blinked tears of pain out of his eyes. He thought frantically about what they could do.

Gregory would know. Gregory always had a plan. Brian looked up carefully at his friend.

Gregory just looked horrified. Astonished.

"Printouts," Darlmore was saying. "Up in my study."

"I did already have a little look-round of your study. When you were out fishing. I saw nothing there. Not related to the capsule."

Darlmore held out a hand to be hoisted. He said, "Hand up?"

"Not a chance, Archbishop."

"The printouts I'm talking about are hidden."

"Where?"

"Behind a bookcase. In a safe."

If this was true, Brian thought, this was a disaster. Brundish had no reason to keep any of them alive once he found the location of the Umpire.

"Show me," said Brundish.

"I can't."

"Crawl." The doctor said to Brian, "Step aside, young man. You're in the archbishop's way. Slump over in that corner. You might as well accustom yourself to being a corpse. In my professional experience, the patient becomes quite relaxed. At first."

When Brian had stepped aside so the way was clear, Brundish bobbled over and nodded his head at Darlmore. The ex-archbishop began a slow and awful crawl across the floor. The man winced with each move. He left a streak of his elfin blood behind him.

With horror, Brian watched the hermit pull himself over to the staircase that led up to the study. He couldn't believe Brundish's cruelty. But he couldn't believe Thomas Darlmore would betray them, either. He kept waiting for something to happen, for someone to save them.

Convulsively, Darlmore began to tug himself up, step by step. His dead leg thumped against the stairs. He grunted in pain.

Brundish leered at the children, then followed the hermit, hopping oddly, as if he, on the other hand, had one leg too many.

They heard him growling at Darlmore on the landing. He clearly enjoyed the pain.

The second Brundish had gone, Gregory started waving Brian wildly toward the back door.

Brian gave a questioning glance.

Gwynyfer, without speaking a word, pointed at the flour on the counter.

In the moments before Brundish had come down the stairs, Darlmore had scribbled three Norumbegan runes in the powder. They read: *BOATHOUSE*.

Brian didn't quite understand, but Gregory swiped the flour off the counter, grabbed his arm, and pulled him toward the back door.

The three of them galloped across the bridge toward the boathouse.

They heard a cry of anger from inside the house. They heard the gun fire upstairs.

"What'll we do when we get there?" Brian asked, falling behind the others.

"I don't know," said Gregory. "Take the boat? Leave?"

"We can't leave Mr. Darlmore!" Brian protested. "Dr. Brundish is going to kill him!"

The others didn't answer.

He knew what they were thinking: that they didn't know what else to do. That Darlmore had given them a chance to escape. That they had to take it.

They slammed the boathouse door open. They ran for the dinghy. Gregory grabbed some of the gear from the wall and handed it to Brian.

"We can't just leave him!" Brian protested.

Gregory threw things they might need through the hatch. "You can't help him," he said. "He doesn't want to

53

be helped." He looked straight at Brian. "Bri, Mr. Darlmore didn't have anything to show Brundish upstairs. He just said that to get the guy away for a second so we could escape. Mr. Darlmore knew that if someone had found the house, there was trouble. He wrote in the flour so we —"

Then they heard a horrible clomping. Brundish was thundering down the bridge toward them.

Brian said, "So we're just going to leave —"

"Yes!" exclaimed Gwynyfer. She was heaving up a can of gasoline. "Now *this* shall be delightful!" She ran out the boathouse door.

Gregory, standing in the dinghy, stared after her. "Don't ask me," he said.

Gwynyfer stood on the little boathouse porch. The doctor hurtled toward her. She shook the gas to douse the bridge. The doctor slowed up and watched her. He raised his pistol. He fired. She flung the can at him.

The thin bolt of blue fire pierced the can, and the whole mess erupted.

The flames were tremendous. Gwynyfer tumbled backward into the boat shed, a strange, triumphant smile on her elfin face. There was another explosion. The end of the bridge was an inferno.

Gregory, swaddled in life jackets, could only look on in admiration.

Through the flames, Brian saw the doctor retreat back toward the house. There'd be no way for him to get to the boathouse now.

So he was stuck there, on the other side, with the wounded hermit. If that final shot inside the house didn't mean . . .

Brian didn't want to think about what would happen to Darlmore. What might have already happened.

Gregory was handing Gwynyfer into the dinghy. He said, "What was that? With the gas?"

She laughed and clapped. "Did you *see*?" she said. "The *flames*?"

The boathouse itself was on fire now. Brian crouched low, because the smoke was thick. He couldn't believe how it dirtied his lungs. He was terrified about the air in the dinghy. It had to hold out for a while.

He jumped in. They were all secure. They slammed the door.

In the boathouse, oars hung crossed on the walls caught like kindling. Life preservers split into flame.

There was a clunk as the dinghy detached itself from the wall.

Another tank of gas caught, and blew.

The shed was now nothing but flames on stilts. The fibers around it vibrated with a strange, metallic hum as they heated. The bridge burned.

Dr. Brundish stood at the back door of Thomas Darlmore's cabin. He aimed his pearl-inlaid pistol, for no good reason, at the flames. They burned and roiled.

He didn't fire.

He went inside the house.

The door banged shut on a spring behind him.

SIX

The Imperial palace had finally stopped smoking the day before. Now courtiers combed the rubble. The ramshackle fortress with its turrets and its chimneys lay in four or five huge mounds, messy welts atop the city of New Norumbega.

On the peak of one of those mounds stood a tall, walking machine that looked like a fortified chair on kangaroo legs. On that striding war-sofa sat several figures: General Malark, a grizzled old soldier with a slice out of his mechanical face; two mannequins from his Corps of Engineers; and, finally, a clockwork troll in the armor of a knight. They looked out over the city.

New Norumbega did not look healthy in the glaring light of the veins above. It had been bombed by the Mannequin Resistance. Its lopsided palace had erupted and collapsed after the unfortunate explosion of the previous Emperor. The tall townhouses of Wednesday Row had holes torn through their slate roofs. The shanties in the Windings were blasted flat. The bronze dome on the

Divine Andraste Theater was crumpled in like green paper. The plywood spire of St. Rugwyth's Cathedral was in a heap. People ran up and down the streets, shouting, making demands. Jeeps bumbled over the rubble.

"The fairest of cities brought low," whispered General Malark. "The walls of chalcedony and gold, the white turrets with their pennants flying, the squares where our masters met and carried on their mysterious trades . . . so much of it's in ruins."

"Never there," said the troll Kalgrash. He shook his head. "Remember: Never there, never there, never there."

General Malark sadly gazed down at the levers that controlled their walking battle tower, the clanksiege.

He said, "So you've told me."

Kalgrash said, "It was always a wreck. Most of New Norumbega was held together with twine."

"I saw the beauty of the city with my own eyes."

"All of us are built to see what they want us to see," said Kalgrash. "I was built after you all left for this world, so they didn't stick me with the razzle-dazzle blinders. I was built by a really good guy. Wee Snig. I just see what's there."

The general looked out over the city of his former masters through the haze of diesel smoke. He said quietly, "Tell us about the city as it really is."

Kalgrash nodded. "It's a mess. Most of it's built out of old stuff. There aren't any town walls. There never were. I don't know what you thought you were bombing, but there weren't any walls to knock down. There aren't any gates. The nice, big houses are made of chunks of dry

57

muscle cut out of the heart. There's no way this place can stand up against a Thusser invasion, not even for five minutes."

Malark pressed his finger to the top of his nose. "The Empress has asked that I defend her city. I can't refuse."

"I'm telling you," said Kalgrash, "we have got to make some decisions."

General Malark considered strategy. "I estimate we have at least two weeks. The Thusser have taken Pflundt, our own fortress down in Three-Gut. But it will take them a while to get here from there. They'll need subs to get through the veins of flux. Otherwise, there's no way to get to the Dry Heart from Three-Gut. Not by marching or land vehicles. It's in a different system. They're stuck in digestion until they can get enough subs to transport their troops up here. And then we'll put up a firm fight before they can unload through the airlocks." He frowned.

The wind picked up across the desert. General Malark activated the clanksiege and walked several gargantuan steps across the pile of rubble. He faced the machine toward the city's black railroad yards. Train tracks stitched their way across the salty plain toward faint red arches of muscle.

"So we have two weeks," said Kalgrash.

Malark nodded. "They're probably running raids on villages down in the guts right now. Trying to find any submarines they can. I'd guess it will take them at least that long to gather a naval attack force. And until then" — he looked around — "we have to fortify this city. Or part of it. We'll evacuate people from some of the farther reaches. Concentrate them. Build a wall out of the flesh. Dig a fosse. Raise a scarp. Ravelins. Redoubts. Revetments."

"I have no idea what any of those things are."

"Of course you don't, troll. You're a machine of peace. I am a machine of war."

"I'm not just a machine of peace. I mean, you know, I smite. Well, I've smitten."

General Malark clapped him on the armor. "Good man," he said. "Good man." He put the clanksiege into gear and began stalking down the mound. The iron feet clomped down spills of concrete and broken glass. Over the grinding of the engine, Malark said, "Look, we're going to need you, troll. We need someone who can see. The Norumbegans will never draw the damn lace curtain from our eyes. You're the only one of us who knows what's lying in heaps around us. We see ruin, too, but of fair palaces and goodly temples."

"Packing crates and aluminum ladders," Kalgrash corrected.

"Stay by me," said General Malark. "We're going to have to abandon some parts of the city and fortify other parts. You'll have to tell us what's really there."

The clanksiege strode across broken towers toward the Empress Elspeth and her Court.

The Empress of the Innards was sitting in a folding metal chair under a tarpaulin held up by planks. Her maids-in-waiting were painting coats of arms on the tarp with poster paints. The Imperial Council and members of the Court sat around her on blankets and towels. There was Lord Attleborough-Stoughton, a captain of industry with a top hat and a ferocious mustache, sitting cross-legged on a traveling rug. There was the Earl of Munderplast, the Prime Minister, a gloomy old man dressed in medieval robes and a velvet cap, crouched uncomfortably on a beach towel. The Duke and Duchess Gwarnmore, Gwynyfer's parents, lay back on a fine cotton sheet smudged with ash. The two of them were dressed for a picnic: she in a white summer dress, he in striped white trousers. A page boy stepped between the blankets, offering cucumber sandwiches.

General Malark, the troll, and the two engineers climbed down from the clanksiege on rungs riveted onto the left leg. They approached the Imperial Presence.

The General bowed. "General Malark of the Mannequin Army greets Her Sublime Highness, the Empress of Old Norumbega, New Norumbega, and the Whole Dominion of the Innards, Electoress of the Bladders, Queen of the Gastric Wastes, Sovereign of Ducts Superior and Inferior, Ruler of All. I come with a report."

The Empress Elspeth did not reply. She was a sly-looking woman with long, gray curls bound up in complications on her head. She wore regal robes and held a scepter. She stared at them all. The girls in their garlands painted sloppy shields on the tent behind her.

General Malark said, "We've been reconnoitering, Your Highness."

She didn't respond. She simply watched him.

He said, "We've been looking at the city, ma'am. We're coming up with a strategy to hold off the Thusser. Big question: how long it will take the Thusser to put together a submarine naval force that can navigate the flux."

The Empress of the Innards did not say anything.

The General continued, "Ma'am, it's clear: The best thing to do is to concentrate the city's population. Gather them all on this hill, probably, and then fortify the jenkins out of the place. We don't have time to surround the whole city with a wall."

The Empress said nothing. The girls behind her whispered softly while they painted.

One of the councilors on the ground asked suspiciously, "General, who told you there isn't a wall *already*? A large, beautiful wall of gold and chalcedony? How do you know that?"

General Malark explained to the Empress, "If I am going to defend the city, ma'am, I will need to know whether there is a wall or not."

Lord Attleborough-Stoughton, frowning under his top hat, said, "Look here, Malark. Those railroads out there are my piece of earth. I can tell you they're important. I want them protected."

Gwynyfer's father, Duke Gwarnmore, complained, "Quite true, Malark. What we really want is for you to defend the whole city. Not just part of it."

General Malark winced. "There's no time, sir."

"Well, that seems awfully moldy for the people who'll lose their homes."

"We cannot fortify the entirety of New Norumbega before the Thusser arrive."

"But, I say, Malark," Duke Gwarnmore protested, "you can't just chuck half the city!"

"It'll be more like three-fourths," said General Malark. And to the Empress, he said, "I am sorry, ma'am."

One of the maids-in-waiting stopped painting and said, "Your Highness, my colors are getting muddy. I think the awful Clarice is dabbing her green in the red pot."

"Am not," muttered Clarice. "Stinko to you, Brendolyn."

The Empress did not respond. Her face was taut and furious.

Duke Gwarnmore drew himself up and put his arm around his knees. "Your Highness, we cannot have this mannequin talking of chopping up the ruddy city. We can't ask our citizens to abandon their homes."

Lord Attleborough-Stoughton said, "See here, I want to talk about this question of the railroads. Those are my tracks, and only a damn fool would try to tell me whether they should be defended or not."

Suddenly, the Empress Elspeth rapped out, "Will all of you keep clacking on when your Empress sits still? I have not yet admitted this . . . personage . . . into my Imperial presence." She gestured at Malark. She said, "He calls himself the general of the Mannequin Army."

"Your Highness," said Malark, "I am General of the Mannequin Army."

"There *is* no Mannequin Army. Not yet, General. There is no separate mannequin kingdom. There is no mannequin republic. There is only one empire, and it is mine"

Kalgrash stepped forward. He said, "Your Highness, does it really matter? I mean, what you call the army?

We're defending you, and after we've defended you, you're going to give us our own republic in the guts. The name — who cares about the name? We have a lot of work to do in the next couple of weeks."

"It matters a terrible lot, actually. Because if *that thing* is called the general of the Mannequin Army, then there is a Mannequin Army. But you are not another army. You are not my allies. You are my own army. You are my subjects. You are my servants. You, sir, are General Malark of the Norumbegan Army, or you are nothing — and until you bow before me, and call yourself General Malark of the Norumbegan Army —"

General Malark said, "Ma'am, we fought to a truce. You agreed to recognize the claims of mannequin independence —"

"Once you won your territory back from the Thusser."

General Malark took two steps away from the pavilion. Then he took three steps back toward the Empress. He said, "Ma'am, I am prepared to defend your city with my life. But until I am recognized as the general of a free Mannequin Army, we will not put one spade or shovel into the dirt — we will not put one stone on top of another stone —"

"No!" said the Empress. "You will not! You are forbidden! Until then, you are an enemy army! An occupying force! Submit to me, mannequin. Bow. Say your true rank: General of the Norumbegan Army."

"This is treachery," complained General Malark.

"It is entirely according to the terms of our truce. You do not become your own separate nation until the Thusser are defeated. Until then, turn a nice leg, bow, and declare yourself mine."

General Malark turned and marched off. His engineers and Kalgrash, startled, looked around at the snickering Council, then followed.

As the chugging of the clanksiege started up and the machine began to stomp away through the ruins, the Empress settled back on her seat and reached for a glass of iced tea.

"Your Sublime Highness," said the Earl of Munderplast, her old, grouchy Prime Minister, "was it really wise to bicker over names with the one man who may defend this city against the Thusser invader?"

"He'll be back, Munderplast," said the Empress Elspeth. "He can't help himself. He's built to love me."

"And who isn't, Your Sublime Highness?" said a doting bishop.

"Exacters. On the button." She squinted at the silhouette of the retreating clanksiege. "I don't like that troll overly much. We can't have anyone telling the manns what's what. Nothing like a spot of blindness to keep them marching in single file." She considered. "One of you kill the troll. Deactivate him. Magnetize him. I don't care. Things will be easier when he's unspooled."

She turned to the side. "Oh, Clarice," she said, "you *are* an awful girl. Your lions look like wombats. And what are they doing, dear? There's a difference between *rampant* and hitchhiking."

She sighed. In heraldry, as in everything else, if you wanted something done right, you had to do it yourself.

SEVEN

The children rode the currents of the blood.

At first, their plan was to wait for the fire to burn out, then return to the magnetic dock.

They waited a long time. They knew that Dr. Brundish would be waiting, too. Brian pictured the ghastly man standing in his grubby robes and top hat, pistol drawn.

An hour passed, or two. They argued about whether they should go back or not.

Gregory and Gwynyfer won the argument, and they all sat tight. Gregory had put himself in charge of the control levers.

Brian sat with his knees up against his chest.

A fan clunked as it circulated the air, trying to filter out the smoke. The kids kept coughing. They'd shut the engine off to conserve gas.

When more time had passed, Gregory and Gwynyfer agreed to go back to the hermit's hut.

But by that time, they discovered they'd drifted. They turned on the electric lights fastened to the hull of the little sub and discovered they were passing through a forest of bloodweed, pushed along by some mysterious tide. They had no idea how far they were from the Dry Heart, let alone the airlock at the boathouse.

Gregory swore. He kept swearing for some time.

Gwynyfer clearly didn't like it. She turned away and stared out another window.

"We've got to go back," Brian said.

"Where's *back*?" Gwynyfer said. "We don't know how to navigate in the flux."

"Against the current," said Brian.

Gregory turned on the motor. The sub chugged along for a while, but the current seemed to have slackened. They couldn't tell which direction they were headed in. They got angry at one another.

Brian pictured the ex-archbishop lying on his kitchen floor, bleeding.

The submarine dinghy chugged through some unnamed vein, moving in some direction, and they hoped they'd run into something that would let them disembark before their air ran out.

After a while, they turned off the motor, turned out the lights, and went to sleep.

When they woke up, they didn't know how long they'd slept. Nothing much was different outside the windows. A school of something yellow scissored past.

"There's the wall of the artery," said Brian.

"Vein," Gregory corrected.

Brian clammed up. Gregory didn't know whether it was a vein or artery any better than he did. Gregory just wanted to correct him. In fact, Brian suspected that Gregory didn't even know the difference between a vein and an artery.

Just when Brian was about to say that out loud, he realized that he also couldn't remember the difference between a vein and an artery. He knew one took blood away from the heart, and the other took blood toward the heart, but he couldn't remember which did which. And he didn't know which direction this particular blood vessel led — toward or away from which heart?

"Do you think we'll die in this dinghy?" Gwynyfer asked, as if she were about to take bets. "I'd be awfully glad of a deviled egg right about nowish."

The two boys didn't answer.

The dinghy puttered on toward nothing. They followed the curve of the wall, seeking other airlocks, other docks, other subs.

Brian was starting to panic. The space was too enclosed. There were only a few cubic feet of cushion, hull, and rivets. The air was getting too hot. The seats smelled of salt and iron. He could tell that there was gasoline in the air. The fan blew raggedly and unevenly. Brian swallowed and coughed.

Suddenly, he wanted to unscrew the door.

Yes, he knew they'd be flooded. But just to be able to move freely . . . to move his arms easily again, even for a few seconds . . .

He knew it was just panic. He knew he had to control himself. But he didn't know how he was going to.

"Do you think there are other Great Bodies?" Gregory asked. "I mean, outside of this one?"

Brian felt like he was about to scream.

Gwynyfer shrugged. "I don't know. I'm not a theologian. There are people who say that if we could just get outside the Great Body, we'd find ourselves in a herd of them, all these massive thingies progressing toward some burning light. And that there would be whole other civilizations inside the other bodies, and we could travel and meet them, which would be jolly." She played with her hair, twisting it around her fingers. "But I don't —"

"I JUST CAN'T TAKE IT!" Brian shouted suddenly. *"I CAN'T! I CAN'T! I CAN'T!"*

He started pounding on the hull. The whole thing wobbled with his blows. He scrabbled around on the cushions. Gregory reached out to grab him.

"Brian! Bri! Bri!"

Brian was having trouble breathing. Felt like he was choking. No air. His breath came hard. He gagged. Grabbing at his throat. Nothing left in his chest.

Gregory was saying something to him — he had to get out — he had to —

Gregory put his hand over Brian's eyes. "Stop it, Brian!" he said firmly. "Stop it. Picture us on a . . . a wide plain. With lots of grass."

"We're not! I can't breathe!"

"Picture yourself. As much space as you need. Sure, it's a little hot. That's cause we're in Iowa in the middle of the summer. Big sky. Big, big sky, Bri."

"There's a gas station by the side of the road," Gwynyfer sang out seductively, and not entirely kindly, "where you can get a double-pack of snack chips . . ."

Gregory insisted, "Picture the big sky. Picture the field."

"Picture the snack chips. Picture the mini-donut gems. Picture the beef jerky."

"All right," said Brian, not entirely gratefully.

They could hear his breathing slow down. They all just sat there. No one moved.

The dinghy dropped deeper and deeper into unknown territory.

And then Gwynyfer called out softly, "As it happens, chappies, we're saved." Her voice was drunk with excitement. "Looky, looky. An extraction station."

They looked out the portholes and saw some vast factory floating in the ooze, a huge assemblage of metal cylinders turning slowly in the currents. Each arm of the thing was capped with a sieve or a funnel. The arms swung past them — or they puttered between them. Huge black shapes wheeled in the green darkness.

"They're run by mannequins, usually," said Gwynyfer. "They get various minerals and things out of the blood. Then they sell them to us. They'll let us dock there. They'll tell us how to get back to the Dry Heart — or down to Two-Gut where the Umpire is. And most important, they'll arrange a lavatory." She beat for joy on the porthole glass.

Then a light flashed on them. It shot through the portholes. Gwynyfer waved. She blew a kiss. The spotlight moved on past, cutting through the gloom. It disappeared.

"Hey!" said Gregory, as if someone out in the bloodstream could hear him. "Where do we go to land?" He

69

steered his way around the facility, looking for someplace they could dock. The whole metal surface of the extraction station was slick with algae, or something like it.

They found a row of hatches of different sizes. There was a small lamp lighting them.

"There are no other subs here," said Gregory. "Shouldn't there be other people? Where's the spotlight that caught us a minute ago?"

No one knew.

With a magnetic clank, the dinghy attached to the skin of the factory and hung there.

The doors were right up against one another. The dinghy slid on grooves until it was locked in place. Gregory shut off the engine.

"Am I amazing at steering or what?" said Gregory. "I could be the star of a submarine cop show."

Gwynyfer and Brian were already stooping by the dinghy's hatch. Gwynyfer said, "Bri-Bri wants space to scream in, and I have to find a little room where an up-and-coming duchess can do the necessary."

They fumbled excitedly with cranks. They figured out how to work a small hand-pump that forced out the watery flux from between the two hulls.

They threw open the dinghy's hatch. With some difficulty, they reached around it and swung wide the hatch into the factory.

They stumbled out into a docking bay, ready for welcome.

But something was very, very wrong.

EIGHT

The docking bay was lit with a dim, bare bulb. The iron walls were scarred and discolored. Someone had spray-painted a Norumbegan rune again and again on all the doors. The rune read: *Closed*.

"No," said Gwynyfer. "A girl doesn't take closed for an answer. My bladder is going to burst like a Christmas cracker."

Gregory asked playfully, "Do future duchesses talk about their bladders?"

Gwynyfer went over and tugged the door handles. "If they don't, they explode into shreds, and then they never get to be duchesses at all."

The kids were unhappy to find two of the doors locked.

But they were even more unhappy, somehow, when the third door was ajar.

It seemed like the place might have been abandoned in a hurry.

The hallway beyond was dark. A faint, clammy breeze blew out of the shadows. Gwynyfer flicked a toggle switch.

There was a long, brown metal corridor. It was lit by one single bulb, halfway down. The other bulbs had been removed.

They no longer joked or talked. They carefully stepped through the portal and made their way down the hallway. Their footfalls made the metal ring dully. It was the only sound they heard.

"Should we keep going?" asked Brian in a voice that suggested he did not think that they should.

The huge edifice was silent, save for the occasional creak.

They walked down hallways and through abandoned offices.

"You know what I just thought of?" whispered Brian. "This place was run by mannequins. I bet they left it behind when they all banded together to attack New Norumbega."

"You know what *I* just thought of?" whispered Gwynyfer. "Mannequins don't have toilets."

And with that, she disappeared.

Gregory gasped and turned.

She was gone.

She'd swerved into a side room. Or had been pulled.

They were worried until they heard her voice. She continued, echoing, "So any little place will do."

She slammed the door shut.

They waited for her to come out.

They stared at each other, leaning against opposite

walls of the metal corridor. They could faintly feel the station turning in the murk.

The sounds from within the side room were very faint. They could hear Gwynyfer walk a few steps.

Then everything fell silent.

Gregory crossed his legs. He and Brian looked nervously up and down the corridor.

Brian was suddenly worried about Gwynyfer. He watched the door. He wondered how long it took girls to pee.

And then, far away, there were footsteps.

They were lonely, slow footsteps, heard through stairwells and control rooms and cold furnaces. Walking slowly, deliberately, toward the kids. The kind of footsteps that might be made by a corpse forced to wander through an endless underworld of empty metal rooms.

Gregory and Brian looked wildly at each other.

"Of course there's someone," hissed Brian. "We knew that. Whoever shined the spotlight on us."

"I don't like this," said Gregory.

Brian shook his head. "I don't, either."

The footsteps had picked up their pace. Now they were jogging down circular metal stairs.

Gregory tapped on the door. "Gwynyfer! Someone's coming!"

She knew enough not to make a joke. She opened the door and peered out. "Oh no," she said.

"Back to the dinghy," said Brian. His face was white.

They quickly — but quietly — padded back the way they had come.

But the clamor was getting closer. They weren't going to make it.

No way they could get back to the sub.

The metal floors around them rang with thuds.

They hid under desks. The three of them were lined up, crouching with chairs pulled in close to their faces.

They did not lift their heads to look when the footfalls slowed. Someone was in the room with them. Someone's breath was fast and thrilled.

They heard the slight clack of metal. Iron things scraping across other iron things.

Out of the dark stepped a man — a Thusser man — with high, pointed ears and the black-rimmed eyes of the Thusser. The orbs of the eyes themselves were wet and dark, all pupil, no white. His face was as round as a baby's. He wore a long Thusser coat but also a harness with many straps, and off those straps hung knives and sickles and jagged tools for cutting and torture. They jingled gently as he walked.

He could not stop licking his lips. His tongue came out of his mouth and squirmed, and went back in and once again lolloped out. His head jerked as he sought his prey.

Crunched up beneath a desk, behind a chair, clutching his own knees, Brian realized: Before they'd left New Norumbega, the kids had heard that the Thusser were trying to seize on subs so they could assault the Dry Heart. This base might not have been abandoned by the mannequins when the mechanical servants went up to the capital to conduct their rebellion. It might have been abandoned when the mannequins realized that the Thusser were coming, that the Horde was searching out all the arteries and veins for submarines of all shapes and sizes to carry their armies.

This lone Thusser, Brian realized, had probably been left to guard this site and trap anyone who landed here.

Brian hid his face. He felt like if he didn't see the Thusser, there was somehow less chance the Thusser would see him.

He saw that Gregory, next to him, was actually shaking with fear.

Two knives rasped together. The Thusser walked slowly through the room. Brian could hear thick breathing as the man licked his own lips.

Brian lifted his head a little. He regretted it: His shirt rustled.

Thump. Thump. Thump.

The legs were right near him. Under the long Thusser coat, the man wore blue polyester tracksuit bottoms. They were too long for him, and their dragging cuffs were wet, smeared black, and torn where he walked on them. His feet were bare, coated in cracked mud like alligator skin.

The Thusser stood near Brian and sighed — a weird, high sound like a little girl who wanted friends.

He shuffled his feet.

And then he dove and yanked the chairs out.

NINE

Two hundred miles away, mannequins were stacking muscle to build a wall. They had manufactured cranes out of wood. They were gouging out the fabric of the Dry Heart to raise up some kind of fort that might withstand attack.

Kalgrash the troll was surprised.

He walked past the quarries, carrying a shovel. He had put aside his battle-ax for a few days until it was needed for smiting.

He found General Malark in a hut, talking with the military engineers.

"Reporting for duty," said Kalgrash.

"Good man," said Malark. He made a couple of final marks in grease pencil on the plans, then rose.

He and Kalgrash went walking along the wall. "Tell me what you see," said Malark.

"What I'm *surprised* to see," the troll said, "is that you're building a wall for the Court at all. I thought you told the Empress yesterday that you weren't going to lift a finger till they agreed to call you the Mannequin Army. And here you are, sir — building a wall."

Malark stopped short, and looked out over the construction. On the other side of the wall rose the ruins of the palace and the Imperial Plaza. Giant chunks of heart jerky were being lowered into place, blocking the view.

"True," he agreed. "I am building a wall." He nodded his head toward it. The wall was not yet very tall. It was pink and striped. "But the Court will have to decide which side of it they want to be on. Tomorrow, it's going to take a sharp turn — *there*. They'll notice that it isn't a wall around the palace. It runs next to the palace. But unless they change their tune, it's going to enclose what used to be called the Easybones Quarter." He smacked his shins together sharply and kept walking. "Our duty is to protect the Norumbegan people. Not the Empress Herself. (May the sun always shine on her radiant face.) So yes, Mr. Kalgrash, we're building a wall. We're raising up a fort to repel the Thusser menace. And we will protect anyone who requests our aid and asylum. But unless the Court sends a petition to General Malark of the Mannequin Army, they will discover themselves to be sitting *outside* that wall when the Horde arrives." He swiveled his head and said, "Incidentally, you're being followed by two young gentlemen. You've noticed?"

Kalgrash nodded. "They seem really friendly. I mean, they haven't talked to me yet, but they showed up this morning and they've been walking around with me everywhere. They're kind of bashful. They keep on hiding behind stuff. But they must have heard about my exploits."

77

"Smiting, Mr. Kalgrash?"

"Exactly. All the smiting."

"Good. But you might want to —"

At that moment, there was a rumble, and everything rippled. The ground shook. People shrieked in surprise.

Malark ducked down, grabbed the troll's arm.

Both of them squatted behind rubble.

"Earthquake," said Malark.

They looked up.

The shaking had dislodged one of the huge blocks from the wall. It was toppling over. Mannequins were running from the collapse.

The block hit the ground with a dull thud.

"What was that?" asked Kalgrash.

"Don't know," muttered Malark. "Let's get back to HQ and find out."

An hour later, they knew. Everyone in New Norumbega knew. Word had come through the radio. All over the city, people were panicked. They didn't know what to do.

For the first time in a century, one of the other hearts had beat.

The Great Body was alive.

❋　❋　❋

Blades swung all around Brian — he ducked — the instruments of dismemberment and torture dangled from their harness straps, slapping together as the Thusser guard pulled him and Gregory out into the open.

Brian scampered back against the desk.

78

The baby-faced guard inspected them both with his black eyes, and inspected Gwynyfer, who he saw crouching still.

He looked back at the boys. His tongue paddled at his lips.

"I am nobly born," said Gwynyfer. "You will want to ransom me."

The Thusser looked at them all again, this time with a terrible, wounded sadness, because he would have to kill ones so young.

He gazed down at his array of cutting and sawing and gouging instruments. He touched a few, as if to remind himself to use them later — where the joints were particularly soft, perhaps, or the bone particularly sturdy.

He yanked Gwynyfer out from under the desk. Wincing, she rose to her feet. She chanted out, "The Honorable Gwynyfer Gwarnmore, daughter of the Duke of the Globular Colon, who is himself of the Imperial Council of New Norumbega, submits to — your grip is rather clampish — listen, I am only submitting to you *insofar as you are a representative of the Magister of the Thusser Horde*. Is that understood? I don't submit to you as a private person. Please state your rank and greet me with joy in your good fortune at so fine a capture."

The Thusser dragged Brian and Gwynyfer beside him and kicked Gregory along in front — the blond boy weaving and toppling, hardly able to catch breath.

Gwynyfer, jerked along by her arm, was still trying to brightly convince the torturer that she was worth saving. "Oh yes, my friend, you'll have a fine tale of honor and chivalry to tell your fellows, as you sit around in your barracks, eating rationed chocolate, playing sentimental tunes on the old upright piano, drinking toasts to the finest — *must* you *drag* so? What is your rank? Do you have a coat of arms? Who is your commanding officer? Take us to him at once! Announce me!"

The Thusser kicked Gregory again, shoved Brian, grabbed Gregory briefly by the collar to get the kid sliding along in the right direction, and pushed them all into a workroom.

Brian seized at one of the Thusser's harness straps — hung for a second — and then, shoved again, he collapsed into the room, snapping the strap.

The chamber's walls were rounded — the inside of a metal drum. There were tables and vats and unlit furnaces.

Brian, Gregory, and Gwynyfer were sprawled on the floor.

The man dragged a huge cauldron and pushed it against the door. It must have weighed several hundred pounds. He'd blocked the way out. He went over to a table and took a machine out of a grubby plastic case. He started to set it up.

Gwynyfer, with a hint of desperation in her voice, asked, "Oh, are you a hobbyist?"

The guard plugged the machine in.

Gwynyfer continued hopefully, "I think it's a fine thing for a person to have a hobby. I may tell you that so famous a man as the Marquis of Holocrine Downsley chisels things into the likeness of bears."

It was at that moment that Brian looked up and saw several Norumbegans dangling from the ceiling.

They were no longer humanoid in their shape. They had begun to spread out into the curved wall, their bodies casting out roots and fronds. The arms of one wound like a growth, no longer straightened by bone.

Brian suspected they'd been captured in a submarine somewhere and dropped off here while the Thusser were performing a sweep of the vein. Now they were part of the place. He'd seen this happen to humans back on Earth: He'd seen how the Thusser Horde anchored themselves using the decomposing thoughts of others to plant their own lush dreams.

Brian looked in horror at those brittle, half-human faces. The mouths were open. The ears were webbed to the metal around them. The bodies slumped into the iron as if they were drowning in bathwater.

And this, he knew, was what the Thusser guard had in store for him and for Gregory and finally for Gwynyfer. They were about to be hypnotized and colonized.

The machine was some kind of projector. It shot out beams and blips of light.

The Thusser strolled over and shut off the overhead lamps in the room. He leaned against the smelting cauldron that blocked the door. The room was dark except for the light that escaped the machine.

It sent out a bead of light. Then nothing. Then another bead of light, in a different direction.

Then a spray of little lights. They darted around like guppies before they faded.

The kids watched the lights warily. They tried to figure out what was going on. They tried to work out a rhythm.

"Don't look at it," Gregory said, looking right at it. "It's . . . This is like what I saw . . . when they captured me before . . . in the dungeon . . . when I had the . . . colors." He kept staring. He did not shut his eyes.

Gwynyfer turned away, her mouth locked shut in fear. She looked up, following a large, flashing orb, and saw the bodies of her fellow Norumbegans fading into the wall. Brian heard her sob under her breath.

Brian was trying to keep thinking. He just wanted to watch lights, not think. He just wanted to count them. He wondered if patterns were repeated, or if all the lights were new.

He saw that Gregory had lain back on the floor, and was completely lost. The blond boy no longer even seemed to notice the Thusser in the corner. He stared at the ceiling and held one arm straight up with the fingers twitching, as if he could play with the bobbling sparks ten feet above him.

Brian knew exactly what was happening. And so he shut his eyes.

He clamped his arm over them. He rocked forward.

Then he heard the Thusser walking over.

He did not open his eyes. Carefully, he hid one of his hands behind his back.

The Thusser put gentle fingers on Brian's arm, and began to pull it away from the boy's face.

For a moment, Brian opened his eyes. The hideous, childlike face with its pudgy tongue stared down at him.

He shut his eyes and then there were fingers on his face.

He pulled his one hand from behind him. In it, he had the strap he'd grabbed and snapped off as he was thrown into the room — and the little dagger that hung on it.

The Thusser pinched Brian's eyelids and tried to drag them open.

The boy stabbed upward.

He hit the torturer's stomach. The guard bellowed — let out a wheeze — and stumbled back. Brian opened his eyes.

The lights were still whirling all over the room. They scraped across the gasping Thusser's wide face.

The Thusser grabbed a curved sword and whipped it out of its strap. His eyes wide in pain, he swung it, lurching toward Brian.

There was a crash, and the room went dark. Gwynyfer had knocked the projector off the table. Brian scuttled into something metal and staggered. He ducked.

The Thusser would be able to see in the dark as soon as his eyes adjusted. Gwynyfer would, too, to some extent. But Brian and Gregory were blind.

Brian heard the Thusser running for him. He darted to the side — trying to make his way to the door, where the light switch was.

The Thusser followed him.

Brian found the wall. He began feeling along, scraping his hands over the rust. There was a crash and Gwynyfer exclaimed, "Take that!"

She must have thrown the projector at the Thusser. Brian could hear the man kicking aside the refuse.

Brian turned on the light.

Gwynyfer was standing on a table, about to throw a length of metal pipe like a javelin. Gregory was on the floor, wincing at the brightness. The Thusser, bleeding heavily, was right by Brian.

He swung his scimitar.

Brian fell back. That was lucky: If he'd stayed on his feet, he would have been sliced in two.

The torturer swung again.

And this time, he might have killed Brian if, three hundred miles away, a heart hadn't beaten, and a pulse hadn't hit.

TEN

The heart that had beat was called #4 (McRiddle's Plum). It was a muscle as large as Iceland. It twitched and collapsed and expanded again, blasting out a tsunami of gore into the arteries, sucking up a rich tide of flux through the veins. The wave of blood coursed through the Great Body, tearing up forests of weeds, hurling dim monstrosities through valves and corridors, slamming submarine boats — and sending the abandoned extraction facility spinning like a jack tossed hard in a game.

Everything was thrown into the air. The Thusser and Brian were hurled onto the floor — then onto the curved wall, where they stuck while the whole base swirled down the artery. Gregory and Gwynyfer were plastered right near them. The metal walls vibrated with the rush of flux.

Gregory had fallen to the wall right next to the half-absorbed Norumbegans. They gaped at him. As the factory tumbled, Gregory found himself rolling toward their vanishing bodies. He scraped with his hands to try to keep himself away.

The Thusser was breathing heavily, losing a lot of blood through the wound to his stomach. Brian thought there was a chance of escaping if they could only make a run for it.

He watched as the heavy cauldron that blocked the door on the other side of the room slowly slid across the floor. If it moved another foot, they'd have a way out. "Come on!" he shouted to his friends.

With a clang, the Thusser struck out at him again. Brian rolled to the side.

The base continued to shift. Machines and tools hopped off the wall, clattering and cascading across the floor. Brian landed and rolled.

The Thusser ran toward him, bounding from floor to wall to floor again.

The Thusser's tongue slapped around his lips and he howled.

The room tilted.

The cauldron plunged toward Brian. He grabbed it as it went past. He rode it as it screeched toward the Thusser. The torturer looked up in panic.

The cauldron slammed into the man. Brian fell off backward.

The baby-faced Thusser was pinned beneath it, his head jerking. He clawed at the kids, but he could not move.

The metal skeleton of the factory moaned in stress.

Brian, Gregory, and Gwynyfer didn't wait to see

whether the Thusser could free himself. They ran to the door, swung it open, and fled the room as fast as they could.

But it wasn't easy to run. Not only were chairs and equipment and stacks of paper slithering up and down halls, but the floor kept shifting. To go straight, they had to climb uphill.

The kids ran for the corridor that led to the docking bay.

Suddenly, they tumbled. They fell through the air. They felt the blows of walls all over their bodies.

They were on the ceiling. Brian gasped in pain. He heard Gregory barking swears beside him as they pulled themselves up and crawled toward their dinghy.

There was a huge collision. Everything shook. The lights went out.

The factory had plunged down against the artery wall. A metal arm had smashed off.

In the complete blackness, they could hear millions of gallons of blood rushing into distant rooms.

Brian and Gregory couldn't see. They were terrified. Around them, the whole huge building pitched and screamed. They didn't know which way to crawl.

"Come along," said Gwynyfer. "This way. Hold on to my heels." She shuffled forward. "Come on! The flux is coming!"

Gwynyfer, who could see faintly in pitch blackness, led them across the ceiling of the docking bay. She shut the bay's airtight door behind them and wheeled its locks closed.

The rushing of waters got louder. There was a hideous iron shriek, and another arm of the factory pulled off. The room jumped. Brian screamed.

The door was creaking. The force of watery blood grew behind it.

Gwynyfer pulled open the hatches to the dinghy. She turned on the light.

The airtight door into the docking bay burst. Flux spouted in.

Gregory and Brian tumbled into the dinghy behind her. They slammed the hatch shut. Brian pulled the lever to lock it.

The whole factory was shifting again — bumping along the arterial wall.

Gregory started the dinghy's engine.

"Release the magnet!" he said. "Cut us free!"

Brian flipped another lever.

The little sub jolted and then was adrift.

Gregory hit the throttle, laid on the gas, and they buzzed away from the spinning factory. Behind them, they could see its greening surface turn and head into the profounder darkness of the lower organs.

Gwynyfer said, "Why, thank you, Bri-Bri, for grabbing that dagger and saving our necks. And thank you, Gregory dear, for lying soundly asleep while it all happened."

Gregory actually looked kind of angry at her sarcasm.

She sighed, "Exhausting." She threw her head back against the hull. "I've only met two Thusser," she said, "Dr. Brundish and this awful bounder with the cutlery. I have to say, I can't recommend them as a people. They seem really rather *moody*. Full of opinions, but with no conversation."

"Where are we going?" asked Brian. He turned on the rattling fan to circulate air.

"I don't know," Gregory answered, and steered them there.

❋　❋　❋

Kalgrash was sick of being followed. He walked along through the Quicknickel Market, casting quick glances behind him. Two men dressed as servants were making their way through the crowd. Both of them wore the livery of the Imperial Court, both had sturdy backpacks, and both were carrying platters. There was nothing on the platters. Kalgrash didn't know what was in the backpacks, but he had a strong suspicion it was not soft bread, fine cheese, and all the makings of a delicious picnic.

Lamps lit the marketplace. Stalls were set up for the night, selling vegetables and flesh. The alleys smelled of rot.

Kalgrash wasn't worried while he was in the market itself. But he could see the assassins getting tense. You could always tell when breathers were about to make their move. Their eyes shifted differently, and their muscles twitched. He could tell that the second he was away from others, they were going to jump. He just didn't know what else they planned to do.

He stopped and looked at a stall that sold kitchenware. He inspected several metal bowls. He stared into their depths. He caught a reflection over his armored shoulder. There was one of the assassins. Kalgrash inspected the man. At first, the guy looked like he was just another servant: He wore the hat, he was carrying the tray, and so on.

Kalgrash looked more carefully at the tray. Then he saw two wires leading from the tray to the backpack.

Suddenly, he knew what was going on. Those weren't trays. They were electromagnets. The backpacks were batteries. The assassins were going to wait until he was alone and then create a magnetic field around him. A light jolt would knock him out. A heavy jolt would erase his memory, his personality. And turned up all the way, a magnet could kill him outright.

Kalgrash stopped inspecting the man in the metal bowl. The girl selling the kitchenware looked at him hopefully. "See one you're interested in?"

Kalgrash tried it on his head. "No. None of them fit. Sorry."

He put the bowl down and stalked away. He was sure the assassins followed.

He turned down Dainsplint Avenue. A building had collapsed into the street earlier in the day, during the heartbeat. Scavengers were looking through the wreckage. Kalgrash kept going.

It was time to confront the assassins.

He found an alley too narrow for both of them to walk side by side. That was important. He had to make sure that they didn't manage to get on either side of him and create a magnetic field between them.

He stepped sideways, suddenly, into the alley, and ran down it.

The assassins saw him dart off the avenue and they moved in for the kill.

The alley was narrow and dark, so narrow the assassins' elbows almost brushed the uneven walls. Their Norumbegan eyes quickly adjusted to the dark. They swiveled their platters so the flat faced forward. Each held his thumb over a switch.

Kalgrash crouched waiting in a doorway, unseen. As the first assassin crept by, the troll reached out gently, quietly, and grabbed the wires that led from the platter to the battery pack. He sliced them neatly with his ax.

That was one electromagnet down — but he'd been seen. The first assassin shouted, and the second assassin rushed to the doorway and faced the mechanical troll.

Kalgrash panicked at the sight of the second assassin's flat, gray tray — soon alive with deadly charge.

He heard a click. A woozy force hit him. It grabbed his ax sideways and slammed it for him into the assassin, clanking hard against the magnet. The man went reeling back against the wall.

The other assassin was still fumbling with his useless platter. Kalgrash grabbed him and used him as a club to beat his friend.

His hands tingled. He'd gotten them too close to the magnetic field. He couldn't work his fingers.

91

So he beat with his metallic fists in clumsy karate chops.

The two Norumbegans were down on the ground. Kalgrash stuck his foot through the loops of wires and yanked. The charge was cut off.

He reached down and grabbed his battle-ax.

"Tell whoever sent you," he said, "that when I smite, it hurts."

He went back out to the avenue.

ELEVEN

Several hours after they left the crashed extraction station, the three kids came upon a docking facility that stuck out into the artery. There were a few subs clamped to it already. Men in diving suits were making repairs.

Gregory steered the dinghy into a berth and shut off the engine.

This time when they stepped through the hatch, the signs were good: A Norumbegan harbormaster greeted them and led them through a long tunnel.

They had landed in a village called Wellbridge, in a side-chamber of the stomach of Two-Gut. The village was surrounded by huge, feathery, frilled growths that towered hundreds of feet into the air. They looked like fungi or molded wax, but they were called gut fingers. The locals figured that when there was food moving through the alien stomach, these structures somehow combed something out of it or absorbed something or spewed something out.

The village itself was carved into the gut fingers. There were windows and doors and even gargoyles carved into the flesh.

The kids decided to stay overnight at a hotel there. There was one diner in town, up in a tower of a gut finger, and they went there to get a square meal. They hadn't eaten for more than a day.

It turned out that the flesh of the gut fingers was the main dish in Wellbridge. The waiter served it to the kids in huge red bowls. It was orange and spongy, and came with tomato sauce.

It wasn't so bad when they tasted it.

"So," said Gregory through a full mouth, "what's the plan?"

"I think we head for the Jejunum," said Brian. "The town of Turnstile. The Ellyllyn Inn. That's the last place the Umpire Capsule sent a postcard from. We need to trace it from there."

Gwynyfer said, "That's on the way to the family estates. The Globular Colon. Wouldn't it be delish to relax for a few days? I, for one, would be glad of a dip in the reflecting pool and a maidservant to rub my feet with pumice stone."

"I'm not sure we have time to, you know, sit by the pool," said Brian. "We don't know how fast time is passing on Earth. Or how quickly the Thusser are spreading there."

"Or here," Gregory added.

"*There's* a terrible thought," said Gwynyfer. "Thusser

94

in my reflecting pool! Here's hoping that the musketry of the Globular Colon was brave enough to keep them out."

They asked the waiter how far it was to Turnstile. He hadn't heard of the town, but he said the journey across the stomach to the intestines, which were called the Volutes, was about four days. Near the Volutes, they'd find the Jejunum. The roads down that way were well marked.

"A few hours ago, there was a big tidal wave of blood in the artery," Gregory said. "Does that always happen?"

The waiter shook his head. "No. Hasn't happened in a hundred years or more. Used to be it happened more often. We'd set the shipping out on the floods and they'd get pulled along. They'd shoot up to the hearts in the veins, come back down in the arteries. Didn't even have to use their engines. But them hearts haven't beat for decades."

"A heartbeat?" Brian said. "That's what happened?"

"That's what's on the far end of this artery. Number Four Heart. McRiddle's Plum. I don't know for sure. We haven't got no news, because the telegraph lines were all tore up when the flood hit. But I reckon it's Number Four Heart." He nodded. "Strange times, milady."

"Strange times indeed," said Gwynyfer, "when a waiter expects a tip and yet doesn't bring a girl's lime fizz."

The waiter flushed and bowed low. Brian couldn't stand to watch a grown man bow to Gwynyfer after she was so rude.

But he saw Gregory grin. He could tell Gregory was impressed by her self-confidence. Her aristocratic command. How much she was already like an adult.

After dinner, they went back to their hotel. It was in another growth. Their rooms were small and warm and hollowed out. They lay down in their burrows, nestled in piles of animal skins, and fell asleep for many, many hours.

✳ ✳ ✳

The next morning, they left Tom Darlmore's dinghy in Wellbridge, realizing they would probably never be back for it. They set out on the sky tram that led off through the forest. The sky tram was a big brass pot they sat in, suspended by cables on tall poles. The pot creaked along, forty or fifty feet above the ground. They were protected from the glaring light of the electrified veins by a paper umbrella. They squatted uncomfortably in the pot and swayed along through the towering gut fingers.

"I feel like I'm a mixed drink," muttered Gregory as the paper umbrella flapped above them in the hot breeze blowing from the Fundus of Dacre.

Every two hours or so, they'd come to an engine station where the cables were cranked by a machine that shot out clouds of diesel smoke. They'd have to get out and switch to the next sky tram for the next leg of their journey.

They passed out of the forest and traveled above a toothy mountain range, the Rugose Hills. The heat from the lux effluvium in the veins above them was overwhelming.

That night, they slept near one of the engine stations. They'd bought food in Wellbridge: more gut finger. They cooked a few slabs over a campfire.

As they cooked, two eyes so deep and green they were almost black watched them from behind a hillock. The kids did not notice.

They talked easily among themselves. Gregory and Gwynyfer had started to call each other G.

Gregory, lying back with his ankles crossed, said, "You know what the sky tram reminds me of, G?"

"No, G. I am simply all ears. Do tell."

"You *are* all ears, G."

"Don't sulk, human G. Someday yours might get pointed, too. You could do it with paper clips."

"Well, G, what I was saying . . . you know what the sky tram reminds me of?"

Brian thought he heard something move in the low scrub. He looked into the blue darkness, but could see nothing.

Gregory explained, "It reminds me of skiing. The ski lift. Has the Honorable Gwynyfer Gwarnmore ever been skiing, G?"

"Why, yes she has, G," said Gwynyfer. "In the Sputum Rifts."

"You know, G, I'm not a bad skier myself," Gregory boasted. "I go up to New Hampshire."

"How nice for you, G. Imagine: New Hampshire." She kicked at a stone near the fire. "Does Bri-Bri go with you to New Hampshire?"

Brian did not, in fact, go skiing with Gregory in New Hampshire. His parents didn't want to pay a hundred dollars a day for the equipment rental and the lift ticket. This year, Gregory had gone with other kids, part of the ski club, and they'd come back with stories of almost crashing into trees and meeting cute girls at fifty miles per hour. Those weekends, Brian had spent his time doodling ideas for his round of the Game — which now would never happen — and practicing his cello.

"No," said Gregory. "Bri-Bri didn't go skiing, G. Bri-Bri was no fun. He stayed at home and did nothing."

Brian wanted to say something, but he was worried that he heard another movement outside the light of their campfire.

"Bri-Bri!" Gwynyfer exclaimed. "Why no fun?"

"It's really expensive," said Brian quietly.

Gwynyfer started to tell a story about a skiing holiday with many noble youths and maidens, the flower of Norumbegan chivalry — a complicated story about running in and out of a sauna with the door flapping — but as she told it, Brian caught sight of something slinking toward their campfire. It was serpentine and low to the ground.

"Hey!" he hissed, and pointed.

"You may interrupt to make a jest or express admiration," said Gwynyfer. "Which will it be?"

Gregory cracked up at this, throwing his head back — then yelped as something darted across his legs.

It looked like a cross between a dragon and an insect and a dachshund. It was long and tubular, and had six

98

short legs and lots of antennae or whiskers. It grabbed their food bag and dashed for the hills.

"What was that?!" Gregory protested. "It ran across my legs!"

It stared at them from a safe distance. They could see its blackish-green eyes reflecting the light of the fire.

Gregory tried to throw stones at it.

It ducked and disappeared.

All night, when one of them woke up, they could hear it munching.

✳   ✳   ✳

The next day, they set off without food. The sky-tram operator at the station told them there was a town a few hours ahead. They could purchase more supplies there.

Gregory was hot and hungry. While they waited to step into the next tram, Gregory said, "Why can't we just call the capsule on the telephone?"

Brian said eagerly, "That's right! There was a phone at the Court! You have phones! Can't we just call down to the inn?"

"Of course we have *phones*," said Gwynyfer. "What do you think we are?"

Brian said, "Oh, I'm sorry . . . it's just . . . just, sometimes the Norumbegans seem to have stuff from the past, and sometimes you have stuff from the future, and, you know, I never know which is which."

"Sorry, Bri-Bri: All human culture is just a dream of Norumbegan culture. We make things, and then you people have some sort of hazy vision of them later and pat yourselves on the back for invention. Your whole culture is just our culture remembered badly."

"That's funny, G," teased Gregory, "because I thought that Norumbegan culture was just our culture remembered badly. You know, G, because Norumbegan culture seems like a big wreck made out of our stuff."

"Human G, that's the kind of thought that gets you a quick, smart slap on the cheek in some circles."

The two kept up their cute fighting while Brian said, "So, Gwynyfer — Gwynyfer? Can't we call that inn down in the Jejunum? In the town of Turnstile? And ask about the capsule? Couldn't we just call down there?"

The future mistress of the Globular Colon gave him the stink-eye. "We have phones. Four or five in the empire. It's not *everyone* who can afford a phone. Just a few of them. One organ to another. For important Imperial business. Who'd want to *chat*, anyway, with people in the Jejunum? Who'd want to know what they ate for breakfast, or what they planned on wearing?"

Brian exhaled. "I thought it was worth a try," he said. "If everyone had a phone."

"Everyone? A phone? What possible use would that be? Most people, one really doesn't want to talk to."

In twenty minutes, a new bucket arrived on the sky tram, and they crawled in.

Brian was miserable. The two Gs were still talking about skiing. They didn't seem to care that their route was uncertain and led toward the enemy. The three of them creaked over the red, rutted terrain with Gregory telling stories about flirting with girls in lift lines. It made Brian feel lonelier than ever. Now he wished even more he'd been with the ski club over the winter. But he knew that even if he had been, he wouldn't have been very much fun. He'd have been falling over all the time and getting tangled up in fencing.

"So I pretended to spill hot chocolate all over her," Gregory was saying.

There was a clank.

The pot swung dangerously.

"What's that?" Brian said.

There was another clank. Something was clawing the bottom of the pot.

A dragon head thrust itself over the side.

Gregory swore and swung his hands around.

"There's nothing to throw!" he said. "I want rocks!"

Gwynyfer lamented, "All the rocks are on the ground!"

Gregory swung a fist, but the thing opened its beak and snapped at him. Then it ducked back.

"Don't!" said Brian. "He just wants food."

"He *got* food!" said Gregory. "*All* our food!"

"So he thinks we have more!" said Brian.

"That's *not* a reason to let him follow us!"

"Well, he thinks it is," said Brian.

The monster retracted its head and disappeared. They could hear it settling itself on the wheels under the bucket.

Gregory peered over the edge. The tram tipped.

"I can't see it. It's way under there." He asked Gwynyfer, "What is it?"

"A heraldic bacterium," she answered.

Both the boys looked at her in confusion. "A *what*?!" said Gregory.

"It's a bacterium. Like a germ. It lives in the Great Body's stomach. But it's heraldic. As in heraldry. Yes? As in the symbols knights wear on their shields and their banners to identify themselves. Back on Earth, we used the creatures of Earth: you know, lions, gryphons, leopards, unicorns, basilisks . . . but none of those creatures live here. So when we have to make up a new coat of arms for someone newly knighted, the College of Heralds chooses some of the bacteria that looks particularly noble as *heraldic* bacteria." She made a face. "It's too *awful*, some of the things the new families have on their coats of arms. Lord Attleborough-Stoughton, the railroad baron, has a kind of a . . . ew . . . some sort of twenty-legged *Bacillus* passant on a field vert — a green background — and the whole thing fairly makes one want to puke."

"So that thing," said Gregory, pointing through the floor, "appears on someone's coat of arms?"

"It's better than most. At least its legs don't hang down creepily."

It stuck with them when they got to the next town. It fluttered up to the roof of the store on translucent wings and waited for them to buy grub. It danced along beside them once they had a few new sacks of food.

Gregory tried to push it away when they got into the next sky gondola. Brian said, "Hey! Don't!" And he held out a chunk of smoked meat.

The heraldic bacterium snatched it out of his fingers, quickly licked his fingertips, and flitted away.

"Now you've torn it," said Gwynyfer. "The thing will never leave us."

It perched most of the time under the carriage of the sky tram. Otherwise, it flew by their sides.

It followed them when they reached the other side of the Rugose Hills and boarded a barge going down the Pyloric Canal.

It slept on the roof of the barge at night while they drifted past fields of alien grains.

It romped beside Brian when they got off at the town of Turnstile to look for the Ellyllyn Inn. He threw the bacterium a stick. It could not have been happier. It pranced over on its six short legs, snatched the stick in its beak, waved it triumphantly, and began to eat it.

Gwynyfer rolled her eyes.

The town of Turnstile was a column of houses and churches and shops that towered above the Pyloric Canal. The Ellyllyn Inn stood off to the side in a grove of weeping willows. It was run by a young couple with plenty of tattoos.

"Welcome to the Ellyllyn Inn," said the inked-up innkeeper. "Your gateway to the Jejunum. May I help you?"

Brian said, "We're looking for some friends."

"Well," said the young man, extending a hand, "you've found a friend in me, kid."

"Oh. Yeah. Thanks. But our friend is three big mannequins carrying a capsule. They're called the Umpire."

The innkeeper smiled. "Sure, they came through. Great guys. Stayed for a week in an alleyway in town, then I let them use the barn for a while. They're off again."

"Do you know where, sir?"

"Sure. They said they were heading into Three-Gut. Mannequin territory. They said they were lonely. They wanted more clockwork acquaintances. Don't suppose you're windup yourself?"

"No. I'm human."

"Well, that's extraordinary."

"They've gone into Three-Gut?"

"That's right."

"But the Thusser are in Three-Gut! They've invaded!"

"Yeah, this was before that. The Umpire Capsule really didn't seem very happy in the barn. Very mopey set of machines. So they're off. Anything else I can help you with?"

"Which way did they go? Into Three-Gut?"

"Through the Volutes. Downriver, then maybe heading off into the side passages at Bloxham. That's where they were heading when they left here. I let them stay in the barn for free."

"How long since they left?"

"Ohhhh . . . maybe three weeks."

"Do you know *where* in Three-Gut they went?"

"They said they were going to visit the town where all the heads of the mannequin people are from."

"Pflundt," whispered Brian. "They're going to Pflundt. It's a fortress. We were there."

"Okay, cool," said the innkeeper. "Cool."

104

Brian said to himself, "No. It's awful. The Thusser took Pflundt a couple of weeks ago."

"I'm sorry," said the innkeeper. "Maybe you should find different friends."

Brian turned to the two Gs. "We're going to be heading straight into Thusser territory."

Gwynyfer smiled. "Unless we sensibly don't go at all."

✳   ✳   ✳

They were back on the barge, heading down the broad canal to Bloxham.

Gwynyfer was bored now, and didn't want to go stomping through the weirder Volutes to stumble into Three-Gut and fall prey to the Thusser Horde. She voted loudly and often that they just continue down through the Volutes to the Globular Colon, where they could spend the season wading in the reflecting pool, playing billiards, and riding thombulants through the pasturelands.

Brian said, "Obviously, we can't do that. We don't have time."

Gwynyfer rolled her eyes. "If the awful Thusser are going to win *anyway*, why not just enjoy the last few weeks of freedom? Maybe by the time we stick our heads out again, the war'll be over and we will have won. Ticker-tape parades and congratters all round!"

This kind of thing made Brian crazy.

He didn't answer. He figured that the best thing he could do was not say anything. If he argued with her, he could tell she was only going to be more stubborn.

105

The heraldic bacterium sat curled up by his feet on the barge.

Brian watched the high grasses go by on either side of the canal. The paddle wheel spluttered. And they drew ever closer to enemy territory.

✳ ✳ ✳

The first assault on the town of Wellbridge came about two days after the kids had left on the trams. Subs captured by the Thusser battered at the docks and forced their way to the landing hatches. Thusser soldiers poured up the passageways that led into Two-Gut.

A Thusser lieutenant stood and watched his men throw firebombs into the graceful gut fingers. Homes and storehouses and the town's hotel blasted into flame. Huge joints of burned gut finger toppled to the ground. Norumbegans ran screaming from the blaze. The Thusser beat them, knocked them out, struck them again and again on their skulls, and dragged them away.

The Horde had come to seize the docked subs. They were building their fleet. Soon they'd be able to attack the Dry Heart itself.

They kicked in doors and ransacked houses. They did not ask any questions. They killed if they needed to. They gathered prisoners for hypnotism.

They did not know that the greatest threat to their invasion was three kids who'd passed through this very town a few days before. They didn't realize that the little

106

dinghy they requisitioned from the docks had recently held the only hope for the Norumbegan Empire.

The Thusser left ten hours later through the hatches. The town was rubble and half-melted gastric comb. It was empty of people.

Heraldic bacteria settled in at nightfall to eat what meat had cooked in the explosion. They blinked silently at each other, wolfing down orange loafs.

A hot wind blew through the forest from somewhere else, and did not stop blowing till morning.

TWELVE

For a day and a half, the three kids floated down the Pyloric Canal on a crowded barge. The towns that passed on shore were ancient-looking places. Their red towers and gables were misshapen, creased, and streaked with black, as if the stone itself was melting. In fact, they were quarried from the flesh of the stomach, which was not as durable as the muscle of the Dry Heart. It decayed faster and drooped, and so the towns of Two-Gut all had the look of antiquity.

As the barge puttered through the lower chambers of the stomach toward the Volutes, passengers got on and off in little villages, driving sheep to market or wheeling bicycles bearing huge spheres of fluff tied with twine. They traded stories of invasion loudly and with fear.

The spell that allowed Brian and Gregory to understand the language of the Norumbegans was under some strain. Apparently, this far down in Two-Gut, people spoke differently than they did in the Imperial Court of the Dry Heart, and so the translation stretched and warped to try to catch new accents and words. Voices ended up sounding more American to the boys now, but, as Gregory said, sort of like cowboys in those Westerns that were made in Spain by Italian directors.

The people sitting on the deck of the barge with their suitcases and their crates of squawking branf told stories of Thusser raids far down in the intestines. The homesteaders and frontiersmen in remote corners of the winding labyrinths that connected Two-Gut with Three-Gut said that the Thusser Horde had sent out brutal expeditions, appearing out of the winding darkness and dragging captives off into another stomach. Many Norumbegans were afraid.

"Where you folks headed?" a woman asked them while she knitted.

"Three-Gut," Brian answered. "We're going to Pflundt. Where the heads of the Mannequin Resistance used to be. We're looking for a capsule carried by three mechanical giants."

"Darlings!" The woman looked up from her knitting. "You ain't smart to go to Pflundt. You going to walk right into Three-Gut, looking like you look? A Norumbegan noble girl — miss, if I can say — and two humans? It's all full of Thusser now. They'll eat you like cheesecake."

Now that she'd said it, it did sound a little stupid.

Gregory touched his head. "Our ears are a giveaway."

"Dag's flush! Of course your ears are a giveaway. And your thinking. We can feel you ain't right. The Thusser, they's sharp as needle-nose pliers. They'll figure you out in seconds."

109

"We need disguises," said Gregory. "Thusser suits."

Gwynyfer said, "That sounds rather jolly. Maybe we could purchase enchantments."

"That's a good idea!" said Brian.

Gregory boasted to the woman, "We've already run into Thusser. One actually tried to kill us. On a sinking . . . factory thing." He held up a fist and flexed his arm muscle. "But we triumphed! Yes, ma'am! Victory!"

He started jerking his head and singing electric-guitar power chords, until Gwynyfer explained to the woman, "It was actually Bri-Bri here who was the hero. He grabbed a knife and stabbed the Thusser. If he hadn't, we'd all have been wallpaper by now. The blond personage there making fists slept through the whole event."

She laughed, and Gregory frowned, and Brian looked at his feet.

A few minutes later, when she got up to stand by the railing and watch the fields go past, Gregory followed her.

"Could you not do that?" he said. "Cut me down? I mean, since we're going out?"

"Are we 'going out'?"

"Yeah. Of course."

She cocked her head. "I didn't think so."

Gregory stumbled back a step. He thought quickly about how beautiful she was, how he wanted to show her off at school, how they liked to call each other G.

He said, "Uh, yeah. Yeah, we are."

She shook her head. "Gregory, we're different *species*. You don't understand what it's *like* with us. Your species *cares* too very much. We . . ." She shrugged.

110

Gregory was stunned. He said, "What? You what?"

She thought for a second. Then she said lightly, "Forgot!" She laughed and scampered off sideways.

Gregory stood by the rail of the boat, stinging.

He glanced over at her. She was inspecting him carefully, as if even the forgetting and the running away had just been to teach him a lesson.

Brian didn't know what had happened. He only knew that Gregory and Gwynyfer were suddenly not being as cute with each other. Gwynyfer kept chattering away happily, but Gregory sat miserably, surrounded by crates of restless branf. He hardly spoke either to Gwynyfer or to Brian. In the evening, he ate alone.

The boat passed the market town of Bury Pete with its green fields of vinch, and later, the cathedral town of Buttercross with its towering meat church rising on huge, powerful arches above the canal. As the barge drifted through the passages beneath the cathedral dome and steeple, Brian and Gregory saw the intricate carvings that had been engraved on the walls there: little monsters embracing and saints floating through the clouds.

A little downriver, they passed a long boat rowed by two farm boys. It looked like it had a whole family's belongings on it: chairs, tables, and a stack of dresses and coats. One of the boys waved his paddle at the ferry and grinned at the passengers.

Gwynyfer murmured, "Look at those arms. Those are true arms."

Gregory demanded, "What do you mean by that?"

She said, "Just, the boy has nice arms."

111

Brian looked at Gregory's arms. They were pretty thin. He wondered whether Gwynyfer was trying to make Gregory jealous. She didn't seem to be, though. She didn't seem to be paying Gregory any attention at all. She gazed out at the farm boy and muttered, "He fills a shirt nicely."

Gregory crossed his arms and sat back. "So what? You can fill a shirt with pig dung." He got up and walked away.

Brian followed him and found him near the prow of the boat. Brian told him, "You shouldn't worry about Gwynyfer and what she thinks."

"It's only a matter of time. The world-famous Gregory Stoffle charm never fails. I just need to keep trying."

"They're not like us. They just aren't."

Gregory snorted. "What do you know about girls?"

"I meant Norumbegans," said Brian angrily. He looked down at the canal for a minute. "You know, you've been kind of mean to me since we got here."

"So what? You've been different, too," Gregory said sharply, and they both stopped talking while the boat puttered on.

The last stop on the line was Bloxham, where the canal broadened out into a huge swamp. The veins of lux effluvium no longer traveled through the roof of the gut here; instead, they wobbled down the walls and across the floor. They flowed beneath the swamp so it glowed a brilliant blue. The town was built on bridges over the electrified veins, illuminated from below. Several hundred feet above, the ceiling was a dull, shadowed gray. Steam floated in the air between the island houses.

From Bloxham, there were portals into the tangle of the Volutes.

The kids walked down the boat's gangplank. The heraldic bacterium scampered along by Brian's feet. Gwynyfer gave the little monster an evil look.

She knew the town. She and her parents passed through it each time they traveled to their estates in the Globular Colon. Usually, she explained, they traveled on from here with a caravan in a coach drawn by thombulants. The caravan protected them from highwaymen on the Gastric Causeway.

She led the boys (and their bacterium) across the town square to the master of caravans. The man sat outside on the steps of his shop beneath a carving of himself. He was a broad man, bald, with a beard. The statue above him, being made of the stomach's rotting stone, had aged faster than he. Its eyes were holes, and its cheeks were pitted and wrinkled.

He saw Gwynyfer coming and bowed his head. "Your Grace," he said.

She greeted him formally and asked him whether they could hire a covered wagon and thombulants to take them into the Volutes toward Three-Gut.

"With all respect, Your Grace, you don't want to go that direction to play your lady games. We've been hearing stories of Thusser. Bad stories."

Hot steam blew across the square.

He suggested, "Why don't you head down to the Globular Colon, as per regular? No reports of anything happening there, my lady. You and these fellows can run down to the Colons and kick off your shoes."

Gwynyfer nodded. "I think that is an excellent idea."

Brian interrupted, "But what we'd like to hire is a wagon to go to Three-Gut."

Gwynyfer rolled her eyes.

Gregory looked uncomfortable.

The master of caravans puffed out his breath. "It is hot," he complained. The square was filled with sparkling, warm mist. "Something's wrong," he said. "The lux effluvium is too hot and bright. Usually, you know, they pump it full of electricity to brighten it during the day. But it's getting so it's overpowering. Just these last few days." He took out a clipboard and made some marks on forms. "Whole empire is falling to pieces." He squinted. "I heard one of the hearts has started beating again."

"It's true," said Gregory. "The heartbeat kicked us, like, a hundred miles down the artery."

The master of caravans shook his head again. "Well, if you want to ride off into the Volutes toward Three-Gut right now, my lady, it's your flaming funeral. But you'd better take everything you need with you: food, tents, everything. Supplies aren't reaching out that way right now. Haven't sent anyone out there for a week."

Brian thought of something, and asked, "Did you hear any rumors — I mean, a couple of weeks ago — of a big capsule of some kind being carried through the Volutes by three giant mannequins? Called the Umpire? They

114

stayed for a while at Turnstile and then came down here and headed for Three-Gut."

The master of caravans considered. "Sure. Heard about that. Some bounty hunters tried to shut them down and sell them for parts. One of the big mannequins turned on them and — I guess threw some punches. Flattened them all."

"Was there any word where *exactly* the giants and their capsule were headed?"

"No one was asking. Big, unhappy things. So. My lady. What can I do for you? A covered wagon and two thombulants? A three-legged and a five-legged? And supplies? Maybe I can interest you in a tent? Or a tent for your servants here, and for yourself, a silk pavilion? With your coat of arms? And cloth of damask to lay on the ground? And you'll want some sweetmeats? And . . ."

Brian didn't speak as Gwynyfer purchased a crazy list of supplies — until she suggested a trumpeteer to announce their arrival in each new village. Then he gently said that he wasn't sure that they needed their own private elfin herald.

Gwynyfer grumbled, "The boys want to rough it."

The master of caravans told them to give him a few hours, and they'd be ready to head off into the low corridors and weird turnings of the lesser Volutes.

"Now," said Gwynyfer, "for disguises. Thusser fancy dress." She made inquiries after local wizards.

There was one enchantment shop in town. Brian was excited to see what it looked like. He'd never been in a store that sold spells before.

Gregory didn't seem that excited about the magic shop. He followed Brian and Gwynyfer by several steps, as if he wasn't with them at all.

The shop was disappointing. The shelves were empty. It was just a big empty storefront with a woman in an apron sitting behind a counter, reading a gardening magazine.

They told her they needed Thusser disguises. Something to make them look like the Horde.

"Going to a party?" she said. "It's all the rage with the kids right now. Thusser and prisoner theme parties. They call it Horde and Veg. With couples, one goes as the Thusser and the other goes as the brain-dead." She reached down by her feet and pulled out three tiny little machines with clips. She went over to a drawer and fished out three little cannisters of some kind to install in the clip-on devices. She plunked the three units down on the counter. "There you are," she said.

Gregory picked up one of the little devices, looking it over suspiciously.

"Attach it to your belt, love," the woman said. "Then click it on."

Gwynyfer picked one up and flicked the toggle switch.

Instantly, she was more dismal looking. She had on a long coat and had dark circles around her eyes, and her eyeballs themselves were black.

"What happened to your eyes?" Gregory said.

"That's what the Thusser eyes look like," the wizard-woman explained. "They only wear normal eyes to be polite."

"*Hm*. That's funny, because I haven't really found them to be very polite," Gregory said. "And what about our, you know, brain waves or whatever?"

"It's a fancy-dress disguise," said the wizard-woman. "It hides who you are. But they'll be able to tell you're hiding who you are, if they ever bother to check. It's more to trick the eye than the brain."

Gwynyfer clicked off her disguise. "Marvelous," she said. "It even makes my hair less honey-ripe and gorgeously buoyant. Which really is a tremendous feat." She reached into her pocket for her wallet. "One wouldn't think the technology existed to de-volumize these golden locks."

Brian asked, "How long do these disguises last?"

The wizard shrugged. "Till the batteries give out, love. Like all of us."

They went to a restaurant and sat at a table outside. They stared at menus. Their silence was awkward. Normally, Gregory would have been cheerful. He loved the adult feeling of going to a restaurant and selecting items off the menu without his mother and father looking over his shoulder. But it was different because Gwynyfer wasn't going out with him. It could have been great, them sitting there together outside and ordering whatever they wanted, and laughing and making private jokes and explaining their jokes to Brian, like they were all in Paris or something, except they were in entrails.

Instead, no one talked. Gregory wanted to ask what "brioche" was, but there was no way he was going to reveal to Gwynyfer that he didn't know a word. Angrily, he ordered breast of branf and a triple-layer chocolate mousse cake.

Outside the circle of sidewalk tables, the heraldic bacterium hopped excitedly from claw to claw and flung himself into the air for little spins on his wings at the sight of their food.

Brian announced, "I have a name for the bacterium."

"You're going to *name* it?" Gwynyfer protested. "Do you name your *body lice*?"

Brian said proudly, "Tars Tarkas."

"Huh?" said Gregory.

Slightly bashful, Brian explained, "Tars Tarkas the Thark. It's the name of my favorite six-limbed character from literature."

Gregory snorted. "I think it's not literature if there are characters with six limbs. That's one of the rules."

Brian said defensively, "And I don't *have body lice*."

Gwynyfer suggested, "Well maybe if you call their pet names loud enough they'll come back." Then she repented and said, "I'm sorry, Bri-Bri. I forget you saved the fam. And us, too. Our hero. We are, of course, frightfully thankful." She reached over and patted his hand. "You can call your vermin whatever you wish."

Gregory gave Brian a hard, knowing look. It said: *You didn't save anyone's family. You accused them of murder.*

Brian turned his eyes toward his entrée.

✳ ✳ ✳

118

The lesser Volutes were a strange and creepy place. The ridge of cartilage surrounding the cavernous entrance was carved into a frowning, fanged face ringed with garlands of flowers. Once the wagon rolled through that gate, the three kids were in dark tubes branching in every direction. At the major crossroads, travelers had carved village names and arrows into the walls.

The thombulants wore huge electric lamps strapped to their backs so the kids could see where they were going. The beasts ambled up and down through the black, looping intestines, pulling the covered wagon behind them.

When they came upon a hut or a village, Brian would get out and ask if anyone had seen the Umpire Capsule. No one had.

They talked to shepherds who wandered through the intestines with their flocks of red sheep grazing on the mosses that grew on the walls. One of the shepherds had heard a story of something like the capsule being carried through the dark caverns of the Volutes, but he didn't know anything more.

They stopped for lunch with the shepherds. Brian had to distract Tars Tarkas so he wouldn't chase the flock. He and the germ played fetch. Tars Tarkas was so happy, his tail twitched with joy. He scampered under the legs of ewes, whirring and clicking with the thrill of the chase. Brian smiled and watched his weird pet fly up and catch twigs thrown in the air. Tars flew back and forth over their heads.

When they were done eating, they left the flock behind.

As they traveled along into the dark, they encountered fewer and fewer Norumbegans.

On the second day of wandering through the Volutes, they came upon a village that had been burned. The huts had been made of junk in the first place: bedsprings, crates, and loose rubble. Now everything was charred. Holes had been kicked in the walls.

No one was there.

"The Thusser raiding parties," Gwynyfer whispered. "Bad show."

From then on, everything they encountered was abandoned and ruined.

They could not tell whether it was day or night anymore. They rarely encountered veins of lux effluvium. The landscape, therefore, was just miles of dark, winding intestine. They slept once. The thombulants slept, too, and blew steam out of their vents.

Gregory sat apart from Gwynyfer. He did not speak much to her. Brian watched them. He wondered why they fought. Gwynyfer did not seem angry, but she did not speak much. None of them did.

Eventually, they came upon a village built on a rise near a bulging vein full of glowing lux effluvium. The vein was fading for the night. The village was made entirely of old rubber tires in stacks, like black, dirty igloos with tin roofs.

No one seemed to be around. Just old machines, abandoned oil drums, and car parts. The wagon rolled slowly into the circle of radial tire dwellings.

"Tars is frightened," whispered Brian. The bacterium

120

was crouched on top of the wagon's canopy, flicking his head back and forth.

"Maybe he smells disinfectant," Gwynyfer said unkindly.

But Gregory was also looking cautious.

And then doors began to open.

Things began to come out.

They were not human. They were not Norumbegan. They were complicated and feathery or leafy. They moved on stalks.

They surrounded the wagon.

THIRTEEN

In New Norumbega, the Mannequin Army was worried. Several of the other hearts in the Great Body's cluster were now beating irregularly, and every six or seven hours, a tremor would shake New Norumbega. This did not make it easy to build walls through the streets of the ruined town.

The tremors also uncovered things. The heaped, broken palace slid and crumbled. One day, a group of mannequin workers moving rubble sent for General Malark. They said they'd found something that looked important.

The general and Kalgrash climbed across the broken expanses of concrete and burnt wood.

"They say it was uncovered in the last earthquake," Malark explained.

Kalgrash shook his head. "These earthquakes make me nervous. Nervous, nervous, nervous. They're getting bigger. I don't like this Great Body moving."

"You should have seen it during the Season of Meals,

Kal. Things shooting through all the passages. Everyone washed away. It was awful."

The troll said, "I'm telling you, we should all just abandon this place. Soon as the Thusser are knocked out of the Game." They climbed down into a pit. "What is it the workers found down here?" Kalgrash asked.

"They don't know. It's a room that was lost somewhere in the palace. The ruins just showed up when the debris shifted."

Lamps lit a cave in all the jumbled trash and the remains of walls and floors.

Kalgrash and Malark ducked and went in.

It was half of a room. The ceiling had fallen and crushed the other half. In this half, there were big, old, yellowing computers, a dot matrix printer, and stacks of old printouts bound into books. On the wall was a poster that showed the Emperor Randall leading off an ice-skating extravaganza. There were cables everywhere.

Kalgrash clicked the knob on a radio. It didn't go on. He followed the cord down behind the desk. It was plugged into the wall, but there was no power.

Malark was sorting through a huge, messy roll of paper that had long ago spilled out of the printer. "Look," he said. "Some kind of messages."

Kalgrash went to his side. Malark held up a lantern and asked, "You've had reading installed, haven't you?"

"Yeah. Last week. English and Norumbegan."

"Don't know if either of those will help you. It's in Norumbegan, but it's mostly abbreviations and numbers and . . . I don't know."

Kalgrash read several entries. They were dated, and talked of the Game. They announced players and winners and losers.

"It's from Wee Sniggleping," said Kalgrash. "Friend of mine back on Earth." He looked down at the mess of wires. "Is there any way to get electricity running through these units again? This looks like some kind of communication center. We should try to get it back in working order."

"No reason we can't power it up," said Malark. "But it will be harder to figure out where all the cables go."

A soldier stepped forward. "Sir," he said. "Nim Forsythe, sir. From the Corps of Engineers. I'm an electrician. The equipment is attached to a long piece of wire that must have been an antenna of some kind. With tiny writing on it. Magical writing."

"I bet," said Kalgrash. "It must have been able to transmit and receive across the barriers between worlds."

Malark considered. "All right," he said. "Let's move all this equipment into our section of the city. Carefully. And nothing gets taken apart without being diagrammed. When it's all set up there, we'll power up and see what we have."

He ducked out of the low passage and went to issue orders.

Kalgrash looked back at the paper readout.

Oct. 12

Round 18 instituted.

124

```
2 hum. cubs (aet. 13/14) engaged via prev.
victor (P. Grendle).


Location: Mt. Norumbega and environs.


Magic within budget (as projected in
summation memo of 4/1). Other ont. parameters
as cited in ritual expenditure memo of 7/6.
```

That was the day the Game had begun. A few months before that, he knew, he'd been built and activated. His memories went back years, but Wee Snig had admitted that Kalgrash was just a little over a year old. He flipped back through the pages of statistics and requests and numbers. He couldn't make sense of them.

But there, in a list on June 7th, was a line item:

```
troll     vacB.328.a   rel 94.16.03


expense 93,983.99
```

He had no idea what the numbers meant, or the abbreviations *vac* and *rel*. He knew what *expense* meant. That was how much magic they'd spent activating him.

June 7th. He'd been born — activated — on June 7. He tried to remember that day. He couldn't recall anything in particular. He was never careful with a calendar.

The last summer had been a good one. Before the Thusser came. Very green, very humid. That summer, he'd done a lot around the yard. He'd sat by the riverbank fishing. He'd made stews out of mushroom caps. Or at least that's what he remembered.

But he knew that one of those many days when he remembered walking to the top of Mount Norumbega for a fresh breeze and a view of eagles, it had actually been his first day alive. It must have been June 7th. That day, he supposed, he'd walked down the leaf-littered path from Wee Snig's workshop on the peak for the first time, and as he'd walked, he'd forgotten Wee Snig a little more with each step, and he'd remembered the warm lair under the bridge which, in reality, he had never seen before.

He had come home after his hike — he thought of it as home, and thought of his walk there as a hike — and he had pulled out ice tea that someone else had made and he had poured himself a glass. He had recalled stirring in lemon himself. That evening — who knew? It had been his first night alive, but it had seemed to him like a thousand others. Maybe he had watched the fireflies come out in the glades, winking like a vast computer console. Or maybe it had rained.

In the dark beneath the ruins, he stared at the record of his making and waited for the engineers to come.

✳   ✳   ✳

Deep in the Volutes, in a town made of tires, heaped creatures stood by the doorways of their huts, unmoving, surrounding the kids' cart.

Brian scrambled to get out the rifle.

"Don't trouble yourself," whispered Gwynyfer. "They're the fungal priests of Blavage."

"The *what*?" said Gregory.

Gwynyfer had already stood up and was addressing the monsters. "The Honorable Gwynyfer Gwarnmore, daughter of His Grace Cheveral Gwarnmore, Duke of the Globular Colon, greets their ancient and holy presences, the fungal priests of Blavage; she requests audience and asylum."

The largest of the mounds moved forward on its complicated, vegetable limbs and gestured gracefully that she should step down from the wagon.

She jumped off and then bowed.

The large mound spoke slowly and softly, as if its voice was not produced through a throat and mouth. It said, *The fungal priests do welcome you, brave animals, kind animals. Come rest. Take water.*

"Won't say no," said Gregory, and he hopped out of the wagon. To Gwynyfer, he whispered, "What's going on? Can you do, like, an introduction?"

She explained, "The fungal priests were here before the Norumbegans came. Not in this sad burg, but in Blavage. It's a spot in Three-Gut they've been living at for centuries. They're famous." She asked them, "Why aren't you at your sacred circle there?"

127

Burned. Fire. Many are soil now. An animal walks in lines and ranks. An animal puts to the torch our kin. We come, bowed and bent, through uncommon ways and the path of nutriment and find now these huts, this haven. We begin again.

"Hi! I'm Gregory. I'm a person. It's great to meet you. Do you ever not talk like that?"

"Their Norumbegan isn't great," Gwynyfer said. "But they're a very popular costume, as you can imagine. More popular than Thusser."

Brian said, "I'm Brian. Did the Thusser destroy your . . . your city or whatever? Your sacred circle? At Blavage?"

The belly fills with dire animals in dark fiber. Vessels eclipsed. The kind machines wind down and stop.

Gwynyfer asked the heap, "Would the fungal priests mind terribly if we stayed here and slept? The thombulants need to rest."

Rest, indeed. We go about our chores. We pray to the Great Body. We pray, for the Great Body wakes.

"Yeah," said Gregory. "We were wondering about that. Why does the Great Body have to wake right now?"

For minds in strife are within it. For there is unrest. For there is anger. It stirs. We pray for its return. We greet its coming nausea.

"That's super of you," said Gregory. "Kids, let's grab the tents and eat the last of the cookie dough."

They set up Gwynyfer's silk pavilion in the center of the village. It had little peaked roofs and pennants and beautiful rugs for her to lie on inside. Setting it up was

128

hot work. Brian and Gregory decided they'd just sleep outside in their sleeping bags. There was no chance of rain.

They sat on their sleeping bags — and Gwynyfer sat near them, on her tapestry cloth of gold — and they watched the fungal priests prepare for the evening.

The creatures danced around the village in the dying light of the lux effluvium. They had no heads, no top nor bottom, and so they danced with whatever branches were closest to the ground, spinning slowly, their fronds fluttering. A rich scent came from them, a hothouse smell, warm and green. This was, Gwynyfer said, their prayer. They exhaled scents to please the Great Body or stimulate it to growth.

Tars Tarkas the germ clearly did not like or trust them. He leaned against Brian, almost wrapped around the boy. He leaned particularly close when Brian ate some branf.

Brian watched the dancing and hated the Thusser for killing and burning these gentle and acrobatic growths. He couldn't stand the cruelty. It reminded him of the bullies who'd poked at his chub in grade school and slapped him from so many directions he dropped his books. It was like a world where those bullies were grown and now could kill with glee, with delight. He was furious.

He asked, "What did they mean about the strife in the thoughts of the Great Body?"

Gwynyfer said, "We don't know if the Great Body has a brain. No one has ever found it. It's possible that instead, it thrives on the thoughts of the creatures that live in it,

129

much, you know, in the way the Thusser use people's thoughts as manure. Gregory's thoughts, for instance. Gregory's thoughts were clearly good manure. A few disco lights and he was knocked out cold and ready to serve the Thusser masters."

"Hey," Gregory said, irked. "Not funny, okay?"

Gwynyfer continued, "So the fungal priests were saying that the strife the Thusser Horde has brought here is like a particularly interesting and difficult idea to the Great Body. Some kind of uneasy dream. It's stirring the Great Body. It might have woken it up." She smiled. "Strife is life. Life is strife."

They fell silent, then, and watched as the pious fungi performed their weird ceremonies at the dying of the light.

In a little while, they decided to go to sleep. The fungal priests were slowing down. Gwynyfer went into her silk pavilion, and they heard her arranging herself on her bed of pillows.

Brian felt small paddling feet on his legs, and realized that Tars Tarkas was curling up on his sleeping bag. He looked down at the insecty dragon. Tars Tarkas's beaky snout was resting on his front pair of claws while his tail and body wound around and around in a spiral. Brian liked the weight there on his knees. It was very reassuring. He liked the earthy smell of the creature, mixed with the deep, forested scent of the praying priests.

He fell deeply asleep.

When he awoke, the Thusser had found them.

130

FOURTEEN

Brian stirred at the sound of wind rustling through leaves. He opened his eyes. A strange voice was hissing, *Meat-children, awake and arise.*

Brian sat up. The high priest of the Blavage fungi stood near them, balanced on one stalk. Its other limbs were sticking straight out in a circle. It said, *They followed; they found us; they are close round about us.*

"What?" said Gregory. "Who? The Thusser?"

The vegetable creature didn't reply, but flapped away. Others were crawling out of the car-tire huts.

Gwynyfer came out of her embroidered tent wearing silk pajamas and a brocade dressing gown. She had overheard. "Well, that's rather anxious-making," she said.

Gregory and Brian were peering down the slope of the intestine into the darkness. They couldn't see any motion.

"The Horde'll still be a few minutes away, I suspect," Gwynyfer told the boys. "The fungal priests will have set out guards. They're all connected by mental roots.

Anything the guards see, the circle of priests here see. We have some time. I suppose we should prepare some defense."

"How?" said Gregory. "We only have one rifle. Do the priests have anything?"

"I think not. They're very peaceable. Poisonous to animals, but peaceable."

The high priest had returned to them. *Flee, friends; away. Leave us to our fate, our final pruning.*

"I learned about you in school," said Gwynyfer. "I'm not going to let you be snuffed out." She said it like the fungal priests were class pets, too adorable to die.

Brian was thinking hard. He looked down the slope into the darkness. There had to be a way to protect the place.

He hated the Thusser. The thought of them burning these creatures and hounding them into the darkness of the Volutes made him feel violent. There was no way they could let the Thusser destroy this settlement of peaceable creatures.

He thought about what they had to work with. He looked around.

Gwynyfer said, "We can take the tin roof off that shed and use it as a gun emplacement. Bri-Bri or I can fire from there."

Gregory said, "Let's do it."

Gwynyfer patted his head. "Sorry, human G. You should learn the Cantrip of Activation sometime. Then you could fire a gun, too. Or turn on a light. Or change the TV station."

Gregory gave her an angry look. "Okay, okay," he said.

Gwynyfer said, "Come along, Bri-Bri. Let's prepare."

Gregory followed them. Together, they lifted the corrugated metal sheet off the top of the shed. They rested it upright against the tires as added armor.

"Now what?" said Gregory. "There must be something else we can do. One gun against a bunch of Thusser isn't going to do much."

The high priest said, *From our sentinels, news: There are twenty of the invader. They shall be here in minutes. They have slain already one of our tender number, a novice growth now laid low.*

The kids looked around wildly. There was still no sign of the enemy in the darkness down the slope.

Brian had been thinking. Suddenly, he said, "Okay . . . I have an idea!"

The others turned to him.

He said, "Hannibal — the guy who invaded Rome on elephant-back — he was in a similar situation. He was surrounded. And what he did was tie bundles of twigs and sticks to the tails of his oxen and light the twigs on fire. Then the cattle all panicked and charged the Romans and set his enemies on fire."

"What a nice story," said Gwynyfer. "Too bad we don't have oxen or some sticks or war elephants."

"But what we have," said Brian, pointing to her and Gregory, "is two pyromaniacs. And some tires."

✳ ✳ ✳

133

The Thusser arrived twenty minutes later. They walked in three rows out of the darkness. Above them, up the slope, the car-tire igloos stood out in silhouette against the dim twist of lux effluvium.

The Thusser sergeant murmured, "If there is one young fungal priest, there will be others. They don't stay far from their own kind. The rest must be up there. We'll have to burn them all. It will be easy. They don't resist."

The Thusser soldiers began marching up toward the village.

And then, with a *whoomf!* of flame, tires began rolling down toward them. Black tires coated in oil and gasoline, lit on fire.

The first few Thusser in the line scampered backward — but not quickly enough. Their long, dark coats caught. They staggered, burning — but more tires were already careening toward them.

Up the hill, there was a system: The priests pulled apart huts, lifted down tires, rolled the tires through a puddle of oil Gwynyfer had spread from a canister — and then sent them spinning on to Gwynyfer or Gregory, who threw matches, kicked the tires down toward the foe, and jumped back. Two by two, the tires tumbled down the slope. Some wobbled to a stop and lay there burning. Others rolled right into the ranks, causing huge confusion. Thusser soldiers panicked and fell back, shoving one another out of the way.

The sergeant yelled orders, and they began to shoot.

Gregory and Gwynyfer ducked behind huts.

Brian began to provide covering fire, shooting his

musket from the side of the village, crouched in the shed. A Thusser warrior fell at his first shot and his second. Then the soldiers began firing on him.

Gregory and Gwynyfer darted out and lit more tires, sent them rolling.

"See?" Gregory shouted. "We make a great team!"

Gwynyfer spared a moment to look at him with pity.

Gregory said, "We were made to burn things together!"

She laughed, threw a match, and said, "The flames of love!"

"Yeah! The inferno of desire!"

"A heart on fire!"

"The third-degree burns of affection!"

Meanwhile, Brian kept bobbing up and shooting. It kept the soldiers occupied.

But in the shadows, a single Thusser soldier watched the kid's head peek over the top of the hut and duck down. The dark-eyed man lowered his rifle and aimed it right at the spot where Brian's face kept appearing. The sniper was going to blow the kid's head up like a cantaloupe. He squinted. He began to speak the Cantrip of Activation.

And then some monster was clawing at his hair, tearing at his hands — a dragony, insecty thing fluttering around his head, snapping with a sharp beak. He tried to knock it out of the air with the butt of his rifle, but the bacterium wrapped its tail around his neck and began to gnaw his nose.

He fell.

The tires kept rolling by, lit up like bonfires.

The battle was over in fifteen minutes.

The last few Thusser had fled.

The kids had won.

* * *

"It is a too delicious victory," said Gwynyfer briskly.

The high priest was not quite so excited. *Soon they shall return. And with some magic-maker, some shaman who shall cause harm, wilt, and blight. We must take us farther in. We must flee. We must find turnings and ways they do not know.*

"You're probably right," said Gwynyfer. "You should set out speedy-like."

She and the boys heaped their things back in their wagon.

Before they had even finished gathering up Gwynyfer's pavilion, the fungal priests of Blavage were stalking off in a long line. They did not say good-bye. They did not thank the kids. They disappeared down the tunnel the way the kids had come.

The wagon, with Gwynyfer shouting to the thombulants, followed ten minutes later. They passed the shuffling fungi. Now the leafy beings raised limbs in farewell.

At a place the tunnel forked four ways, the kids went one way and the priests went another. All were swallowed up in darkness.

For hours, the kids forced the thombulants to canter as fast as the beasts could go. The thump of those gigantic feet, the splash through rivers of half-digested ooze —

these things were the only sounds the three heard. All they saw were ragged circles of gray picked out by the thombulants' spotlights. They were joggled by the cart flying over the rough floor of the tunnel.

They took crazy turnings, trying to make sure they were as hard to follow as possible.

When they stopped to eat and rest many hours later, they were exhausted.

They sat in the wagon, leaning on all their gear. They chewed on dried meat and fruits.

Gregory poked at Gwynyfer with a dried apricot. "So, you agree that we make a good team."

"I agree."

"A *really* good team. Almost like we're meant to be together."

Gwynyfer pushed his hand and his apricot away. "Stop congratulating yourself," she said. "Let's talk about Bri-Bri for a tick. He's the real hero. He's the one who came up with that delightful plan with the burning tires. And the elephants, though I got somewhat lost at the elephants."

From her voice, it did not sound like she was praising Brian to be nice. It sounded instead like she was praising him to make Gregory angry.

She reached out and ran her fingers through Brian's hair. "You know, I think maybe we should record Bri-Bri's heroic deeds in song. Oh, for a lute! I'd strike out chords, and, Gregory, you could wear tights and sing, 'Brian, Brian, fa la la. Brian, Brian, he's the best. Fa la la.' Et cetera."

137

"All right," said Gregory miserably. He stood up. "I'm going to walk around for a minute."

Brian ducked to get Gwynyfer's hand off his head.

But Gwynyfer kept talking. "And Brian was the one who grabbed that knife from that terrible man in the factory. It was too very brave, don't you think? He thought of it wonderfully quickly. And all the while, there you were, Greggers, staring into the light like a run-down mannequin."

"I've heard it before," said Gregory. He clambered out of the wagon.

"And Bri-Bri figured out who the murderer was. He figured out that the Emperor was a radio or a bomb or a bomb on the radio or whatever the Emperor was. He worked out the whole thing, which is frightfully clever, especially given that he's really rather timid and maybe dim.

"And Bri-Bri was the one who saved my parents when they were accused of murder. Bri-Bri was the one who figured out who was scheming things up with our explosive Highness and he so bravely stepped forward to speak the truth when all the Court wished very hard to pinch him and throw him off the balcony. Thank you, Bri-Bri." She kissed Brian on the cheek. "Bri-Bri was the one who —"

At this, Gregory snapped. He yelled, "No, he isn't! No, he isn't the person who saved your parents!" He pointed his finger at Brian, who looked like he wanted to shrink into a hole. *"He's the one who accused them in the first place! Okay? You hear me? He's the one who said to me* that you were in on the murder! He thought you were a spy! He thought your father stabbed the Regent!"

Gwynyfer stopped in the middle of her speech. She swiveled her head to stare at Brian.

"True, Bri-Bri?" she asked.

He sat sheepishly, unable to answer. He said, "I, uh — you could . . . I was wrong about . . ."

"True, Bri-Bri?"

Brian said, "But I was wrong! I thought so, but only as one, you know, possible thing. With lots of other possibilities."

Brian could actually see Gwynyfer's face fill with rage.

"You thought my father had committed the murder?"

"No, I —"

"Yes," insisted Gregory. "He did."

"I don't *believe* you!" Gwynyfer said to Brian. "I don't *believe* you hid that from me! You could have had us thrown off the tower! My whole family! You really are a vile little worm! I take back my lute song! You're a pale, ugly, sneaky little lickspittle!" She flung herself to her feet, stooping beneath the bonnet of the wagon, and started kicking Brian's shins. "You're a hateful creep! A friend of bacteria! And machines! Your only friends — yes! — your only friends are mannequins and filth!"

Brian was trying to defend himself. He tried shouting, but she shouted louder.

"I *hate* you!" she screamed.

"Hey!" Gregory hissed. "Quiet! The Thusser! We don't know how far away they are!"

139

She remembered where she was. She fell silent, but her eyes were still burning.

She sat down across from Brian.

She stared at him.

"Sleepy?" she asked.

He blinked back, but didn't have anything to say.

She kept staring and waiting.

He moved to feed Tars some jerky.

Gwynyfer swiftly kicked it out of his hand. "You're not going to feed that *thing* our food," she said. "Tell it to go away!"

Tars, bunched up on the seat, looked confused.

Gwynyfer still stared at Brian. He didn't reach for more jerky.

For the next several hours, they all thought about sleeping. But Gwynyfer would not let them. When Brian, miserable, would begin to droop, Gwynyfer would lash out violently at his ankle. *"Traitor!"* she'd say.

He'd sit up and shift.

And so they spent an awful, wakeful time just sitting there, all half dazed with weariness. No one bothered to take out the sleeping bags or put away the food. They rested on mounds of supplies. Brian slid down next to a barrel of water.

"Don't sleep, porky!"

Brian turned away. He was ashamed that he wanted to cry.

"Think about what you did."

He felt a touch on his back. It was Tars. The creature crawled next to him. Brian heard Gwynyfer cough with disgust. Tars put his claw on Brian's neck and curled his long tail around Brian's arm.

She's right, he thought to himself. His only friends were bacteria and machines.

In that moment, it felt like Tars was his only friend in the world. He leaned his head against Tars's stomach.

Finally, they all couldn't hold their eyes open any longer. They passed to sleep.

By the next night, they would no longer be together.

FIFTEEN

Several hours later, Gwynyfer somehow remembered she was supposed to be glaring, and woke herself up.

Brian was curled next to the water cask. Gregory was asleep on top of their folded tents. Everything was dark.

Gwynyfer kicked out at Brian's ankle again.

"Ah!" He jolted up and slammed his head on the water.

She glared at him. He looked around frantically.

She remembered that he couldn't see in the dark. She reached out and touched a lantern. She muttered the Cantrip of Activation. It lit up.

She faced Brian again and took up her glaring.

"Look," he said, "I'm sorry. But we have to . . . I had to think about all the possible suspects. And your —"

"Stick a sock in it."

Brian stopped talking.

Gregory sat up. "What's happening?" he said. "Did any of us keep watch last night?"

"No," said Gwynyfer. "It's Brian's fault."

Brian started to protest, but Gregory shouted louder, "Our food!"

They looked over at their food supply. The bags had been torn open and bits of brown paper were smeared all over the place. Gregory leaned over and looked through the bags. The meat was gone. The vegetables were scratched to pieces. The cereal was all over the place.

Gwynyfer shouted, "That little vermin! Your little monster!" She shoved Brian in the shoulder.

"Hey!" he said. "You wouldn't let me feed him!"

She stuck her head out of the wagon's bonnet. "Not a *sign* of it! It flew the coop! Great Manannan! I'd like to wring its chitinous *neck*!" She popped back in. "And don't you tell me this happened because I didn't let you feed it! We'd still have a wagon full of food if you hadn't petted a *bacterium* and coaxed it and made googly eyes at it, and convinced it we wanted nothing more than for a piece of six-legged *filth* to crawl along with us!"

Brian was stinging. He was furious with Gwynyfer, but afraid of her. And he couldn't believe that little Tars had turned on him like this — just eaten everything and run. At the same time, he knew it was true. They should have put the food away, but they hadn't. And Tars didn't know right from wrong. He just knew salted from unsalted.

Gregory still was going through the food bags. "There's almost nothing left," he said. "If Tars didn't eat it, he ruined it." He made a disgusted noise. "It looks like he ate the fish while he sat in the onion dip." He put his hand over his mouth. "There's a butt-print."

143

They had to get ready and keep going. They all knew it. The Thusser would be sending out more search parties through the Volutes.

"So now," said Gwynyfer as she harnessed the thombulants, "we have to go into Three-Gut — into Thusser territory — with absolutely no food and nothing to protect us but a few party costumes. This really is ripping."

She climbed into the wagon and set the thombulants walking.

"Topping," she said.

Brian sat, meek and miserable, in the back of the wagon. He looked into the darkness, hoping he'd see a glimmer of Tars Tarkas's eyes. He felt guilty and angry all at once.

The other two hardly talked to him. They passed through burned-out villages. Now they were close enough to Three-Gut that the villages had belonged to the mannequins. They saw a few smashed clockwork people who had tried to resist as the Thusser swept down from the stomach.

Now Gwynyfer leaned against Gregory and held his hand. Brian could hear her laughing at Gregory's jokes. Brian could tell that Gregory wasn't standing up for him.

They were approaching the stomach of Three-Gut. A wind blew through the tubes.

Everyone was starving, but there was nothing to eat but fragments of flatbread and cucumbers with claw marks in them.

Brian sat dolefully, munching half of a green pepper.

They didn't have any food left for dinner.

After they'd been traveling ten hours with Brian hiding, disgraced, in the back of the wagon, Gregory and Gwynyfer decided they wanted to stop to rest. The thombulants were tired. They stopped by a huge statue of St. Miach, the patron saint of the mannequins. He had a halo and was holding a platter of replacement hands.

Gwynyfer clambered down and went to tie the beasts up.

Brian approached Gregory. He just said, "Gregory . . ."

Gregory looked at him but didn't say anything.

Brian couldn't even finish his sentence. Instead, he murmured, "I'm going to go off and go to the bathroom."

He climbed down and wandered off into the dark, carrying a lantern.

Gwynyfer looked up from the thombulants. She saw Brian's light receding, stopped what she was doing, and began harnessing the beasts again. When she was done, she ran back and climbed up.

"Where's your greasy, chubby little friend going?" she asked Gregory.

"Whiz."

Gwynyfer smiled at Gregory, pinched his cheek, and shook the thombulants' reins.

"What are you doing?" said Gregory.

"Prank," said Gwynyfer. "Imagine when he gets back and we're gone."

"You can't just leave him!"

"We're coming right back!" She giggled with her lips very close to Gregory's face. She whispered, "Cowardy custard."

145

Suddenly, she slapped the thombulants and they flew forward. Gregory almost tumbled backward. "Whoa!"

She started laughing, so he started laughing, and soon they were laughing together.

When they had gone about a quarter of a mile, Gregory said, "Okay. Okay, G. Stop. Let's wait here. We'll give it ten minutes, then go back."

"Why *wait*?" said Gwynyfer. She kept going. "G, we're not going back for Mr. Thatz at all. Off instead to the scenic Globular Colon! For lovely afternoons spent bathing and eating strawberry ices."

Gregory hoped she was joking. He made a kind of stiff laughing sound. "Sure," he said.

"You know, G, you have not always the spirit of waggish fun one likes to see in a boy."

"But, I mean, we're going back for Brian, right?"

"So he can look tense and wounded while we do Ping-Pong tournaments? I think not."

"Gwynyfer . . ."

"Do you think we should go left here?"

"We've got to turn around."

"Indeed we do, to avoid that smelly, old Three-Gut. But if we turn around here, see, we'll run into Bri-Bri."

"We can't just leave him!"

"You're the living end."

"We can't!"

"Was he ever fun? No, G, he was not. No hoot was he."

"He's sitting back there, thinking that we abandoned him!"

146

"And he's not wrong! Do you want your friend to be wrong? No. We like him to be right. So do we go left? Or straight on? Tell your fetching charioteer."

"*Gwynyfer!*" Gregory shouted. "Brian is my friend! I know you don't like him! But he's my friend! And we're going back right now! I can't believe you'd actually abandon him."

She slowed the thombulants. She was thoughtful. "This is too bad," she said. "Really too bad. I thought I'd found my equal in you." She started to turn the thombulants around. "But you, too, when push comes to shove, are a drip. A safe little boy. A human."

She shook the reins. The thombulants began pacing back up the tunnel toward Brian.

Gregory said, "Gwynyfer . . . you know I like a joke."

Gwynyfer shrugged. "It was just an idea," she said. "Just a little idea."

They rolled back toward the statue of St. Miach and his dish of hands.

✳   ✳   ✳

Brian stood amazed, looking at the statue of St. Miach picked out in his lantern. The stone face gazed down at him, kind and concerned. Brian was sure this was where the wagon had been. There was no sign of it now.

He walked a ways down the tunnel. Nothing.

He went back to the roadside shrine of St. Miach. His stomach was falling.

They hadn't abandoned him. They couldn't have. Gregory was acting like a jerk sometimes lately, but he wouldn't do that to his best friend.

Then he thought about the way Gregory had been behaving the last year in school. A lot of times, he did stuff without Brian. He went off with cooler friends.

And Gwynyfer . . . Brian knew she was, at heart, a Norumbegan, and that meant she could never be trusted. They didn't feel things the way humans did.

Brian, leaning against the saint's robed knee, felt supremely sorry for himself. There he was, alone in the tunnel, close to a vast, empty stomach, facing a world of unknown terrors. He didn't even have his gun.

He heard a clank.

They were back. It had been a joke. A stupid joke. He stood up and shouted, "I can't *believe* you'd just go off like that! It's not funny!"

"So sorry," said a voice. "We promise we won't leave you again."

The figures filed into the light from Brian's lantern.

Men in dark, long coats; men with black eyes.

He did not have a chance to run.

SIXTEEN

Gregory stared astounded at the statue of St. Miach in their headlights. Brian was not there.

They had searched farther up the tunnel. Nothing. No one.

"Pity," said Gwynyfer. "Now off to the Globular Colon!"

"We've got to stay here in case he comes back," said Gregory.

"Comes *back*? I don't, frankly, think that's going to happen. He couldn't have just wandered off. Someone with a thomb or a carriage must have picked him up. He's gone, G."

"What are you saying?"

"He wanted to go to Pflundt. Why, he's doubtless well on his way by now. With a whole new set of glittering Thusser friends."

"You think he's a prisoner?"

"Oh, or dead. How do you expect me to know? Don't be trying. Now there're more food scraps for the rest of us. Bags I the carrot heel."

Gregory demanded they wait by the statue. For hours, they sat there. Gwynyfer was furious.

Brian did not return. Gregory felt an awful, growing certainty that the whole time they were sitting there, Brian was getting farther and farther away.

After a while, Gregory said it was time to give up and start hunting for him.

Gwynyfer didn't agree. "Is it really that time? I would a good deal rather we do our grieving — so young, so sad — and then move on to the portion of the week where we swim and go downhill skiing."

"We'll go this direction," said Gregory. "Back where we came from originally. He obviously didn't pass us in the tunnel, so whoever took him must have gone back that way."

They rolled down the corridor, shouting Brian's name. There was no answer. They reached a fork in the intestine. They did not know which way to go. They followed another route that led toward the stomach of Three-Gut.

They saw they were coming to another one of the burnt villages. This time, there were figures moving about there.

"Thusser," whispered Gwynyfer. "Get the disguises."

Gregory slipped back and grabbed their little metal cloaking devices. Brian's was right there beside the other two. Gregory shook his head. He couldn't believe Brian had left his disguise behind. He handed one to Gwynyfer. They flicked the switches.

150

Immediately, they were Thusser. Their eyes were black, they wore long military coats, and Gregory's ears now were pointed.

Cautiously, they rolled into the village. It had been turned into a depot for the Thusser Horde. Soldiers went past in lines, carrying camera-like devices on long poles.

Men looked up at the two kids, but they did not excite attention. Gregory and Gwynyfer rode slowly through the village. They stared straight ahead.

In one of the burned-out houses, now just a few portions of brick wall, Brian Thatz looked up from his torture. He opened his eyes, panting. He was sitting on the ground with his wrists and ankles shackled behind him.

He saw his wagon.

He saw Gregory and Gwynyfer looking like Thusser.

The wagon was just going past. It didn't stop.

He started to shout Gregory's name.

And then the Thusser torturer touched Brian's forehead again and said magical words, and pain seared along the boy's every vein. He felt like his skin was burning off. He felt the muscles sear. He rolled on the ground, slamming his head against the bricks again and again to make the pain stop.

The wagon was gone. Gregory and Gwynyfer hadn't seen him.

The wizard clapped and the pain ceased. Brian collapsed. His head was bleeding where he'd hit it against the wall.

"Please don't . . . again . . ." he said.

The wizard did not speak to him.

The wagon was out of town.

"Well," said Gwynyfer, "thank goodness our disguises held. That was really rather nervous-making. But here we are, on the other side."

Gregory nodded.

They rode on toward the stomach of Three-Gut.

✳ ✳ ✳

In the dark hills of Vermont, the Thusser worked all night. Troops and machines rumbled out of the red, angry hole that led to their world from the center of a warped suburban lawn. Platoons of soldiers marched through the streets in their long, black coats. The houses that lined the avenues were Thusser nests, moving gently and sweetly in the light breeze. Occasionally a corner or a roofline of a human house would catch the white, shifting fabric of the nests. There was no sign of the human owners, though. They were sunk deep within their homes, dreaming. Thusser families stood on their lawns, watching the soldiers pass.

In the City of Gargoyles, far beneath Norumbega Mountain, army formations were on the move. They manned the battlements of the old Imperial palace. They waited in the square outside the gates of St. Diancecht's cathedral. Upon orders, they marched through the dark nave of the cathedral. Their boots clapped loudly on the stone floor. They marched down the steps to the crypt. There, past the tombs of all the dead kings and emperors of

Norumbega, lay the doorway to the Great Body. Thusser streamed through. Wizards clutched the edges of the black portal between worlds, exhausting themselves to keep it open and to send so many bodies passing through.

For twenty or thirty miles around that spot, Thusser skulked through the streets of small Vermont villages. They set up tall poles that broadcast thought and that sped up time.

People sleeping in their beds had strange dreams and did not protest when figures crawled through their windows.

A man stood by his refrigerator, mouth open. He was in a T-shirt and boxer shorts. The refrigerator door was open, and the light inside was bright, reflecting off the plastic of cheeses, the cling wrap around gray meat, and a six-pack of beer. He did not move. A Thusser man sat at his table, whispering to him in words no human could understand.

On Interstate 89, there were few cars. A girl rode in the back seat of one of them, half asleep. Her mom and dad were taking her to Montreal. Her dreams were troubled. She could not get out of her head scenes of men with blackened eyes. She opened her eyes, dropping the book she had been reading earlier.

Fir trees and pines ran in a jumble past the car windows. The lone car's headlights lit the dotted lines for lanes in regular rhythm.

Distant mountains glowed under a partial moon. The car was passing the exit for a town called Gerenford.

Suddenly, there was a man standing by the side of the

road. He did not wave his arms or try to hitchhike. And yet the girl saw her father slow down, put on his blinker, and start to pull over.

"Andy, don't," said the mother. "What are you doing?"

He came to a stop. The man in the long coat walked to their car.

The mother locked her door.

The father stared straight ahead.

"Andy, lock the doors. Lock the doors!"

The girl scrambled to click the locks in the backseat, but the man in the long black coat had already strolled to her father's door and opened it. He waited while the father got out.

The girl stared frantically into the front seat — wondering whether to stay in the car or to run — but her mother shouted, "Duck, Carlie!" and threw herself over into the driver's seat to slam the door shut and lock all the doors automatically. "Andy!" the mother screamed. "What's going on?"

Now there were more of the men coming out of the woods.

The father stood without moving.

The car was surrounded by men and women with black marbles for eyes. They came closer. They touched the metal of the car, the glass of the windows.

Helplessly, the mother reached forward, whispering, "Don't . . ."

"Mom?" said the girl.

The mother was staring straight ahead. She touched a

button, and with a clunk, all the doors in the car unlocked at once.

The little girl started to yell.

✳ ✳ ✳

Two hours later, there was a traffic jam on the highway. It looked like a traffic jam, but it was silent. The cars were empty. Their headlights were on. Their engines were off. Their doors were open, where people had been dragged out. Soldiers in long black coats carried them on stretchers off into the woods.

The girl stared into the trees flowing above her. She could not remember a time when she had not been carried like this by men and women in long, dark coats with black marble eyes. She would always be carried. There would always be branches above her. There would always be part of a moon.

She closed her eyes happily and went to sleep.

SEVENTEEN

A day after Brian disappeared, Gregory and Gwynyfer emerged from the Volutes and found themselves in the great stomach of Three-Gut.

Far above, the gray, cavernous ceiling was broken by the dull, glowing veins of the lux effluvium. Flat, swampy plains stretched far into the distance. Around the entrance to the intestines, there was a small village of crumbling brick. It was now occupied by a few Thusser who sat in lawn chairs, smoking cigarettes and tapping the ash into a rusted coffee can.

They raised their hands as Gregory and Gwynyfer, disguised, went past.

There was a single causeway that led off into the marshy distance. Gregory and Gwynyfer followed it, since that was the only way to go; they didn't have one of the sleighs that mannequins drove straight across the sea of muck.

The wagon rolled slowly along the causeway. Gwynyfer

didn't bother steering. She was bored and angry and sat with her arms crossed.

Once they crossed paths with a small detachment of Thusser soldiers riding in wagons. Gwynyfer and Gregory clicked on their disguises. They waved and pulled to the side of the road. The soldiers saluted them and drove on toward the entrance to the Volutes.

Both the kids were starving. They had barely eaten anything for a whole day. Gregory couldn't sleep because he was too hungry.

Just as the veins were beginning to lighten, they came to a tall, gabled inn that rose up beside the causeway. They stopped for a meal. Before they went in, they made sure they were disguised.

"You look awful," Gwynyfer said playfully.

Gregory was in no mood to play. He didn't say anything.

The taproom was paneled in dark wood, or something that looked like it. A square-shaped Thusser with short, silver hair scrubbed mugs and whistled.

"Food," said Gwynyfer. "I could fairly kill for an omelet."

The man stopped scrubbing and looked them up and down skeptically with his black eyes. He did not speak. Gregory worried their costumes weren't convincing enough.

"Are you the innkeeper?" Gwynyfer said, trying to be brave. "This is your inn?"

The man clearly thought about whether he should be welcoming and generous.

Gwynyfer prodded, "This inn belongs to you, sir?"

The man nodded. "The longtime owners were mechanical, and suffered an unfortunate technical failure last week while down in the extensive cellars."

"A technical failure?"

"In this sad life, we can be sure of nothing. I fear to say I happened to be present at the couple's demise. It was very sad and grisly. They will be much missed. But, children, it will be my utmost pleasure to serve you. Or, rather, since you appear to be still in the bloom of freshest youth, it will be my pleasure to serve your parents, whenever they arrive." The innkeeper waited with crossed arms. He clearly was not going to serve a couple of unaccompanied kids, perhaps runaways.

Gwynyfer reached into her pocket and pulled out several gold coins. "Our parents," she said, putting them on the counter.

The innkeeper smiled. "The young woman comes of good stock," he said. "It is a pleasure to make their acquaintance." He picked up one of the coins. "Norumbegan kroners. One doesn't often see these. Outside of Norumbega." He smiled.

Gwynyfer slid the coins back toward her. "If you'd like to argue with our parents, they'll take us elsewhere for breakfast."

"No, no, mademoiselle! I'd be delighted to serve you and your — your brother?"

"That will do."

They were starving. They ordered a pile of food to eat immediately and quite a lot to take with them. Gregory

158

sat silent and miserable while they waited. Gwynyfer talked happily and inspected the photos of mechanical rowing teams on the walls.

The innkeeper came back in a few minutes with plates. He smiled and watched them eat with his hands clasped behind his back.

"In this business," he said, "one meets so many fascinating types from all over the many worlds of the Thusser dominion. I count myself lucky, as I am somewhat of a 'people person.' How unusual, for example, to encounter two unaccompanied children in a war zone who use Norumbegan coin and speak with a pronounced Norumbegan court accent, and who shield their thought emanations from all and sundry, as if they had something to hide. It almost causes the humble student of Thusser character to ask: Why? And wherefore?"

"Is it unusual?" said Gwynyfer. "Is it really that unusual for Thusser children born with exceptionally strong magical gifts of a startlingly violent, destructive nature, to find their parents irritating, even meddling, and to finish the goofs off with a quick explosion of blaring demon-fire? And then to set out on their own?" She smiled. "One reads of such things in the paper."

At the mention of blaring demon-fire, the innkeeper started to look a little nervous. He replied, "Of course, not unusual at all. No, no, mademoiselle. Children will have their little pranks. I always say that a little patricide and matricide prepares one for marriage. As long, you know, as you keep it in the family."

"I agree," said Gwynyfer. "Much better not to spend

159

our precious gifts of destruction on passing strangers. And we would never think of doing so, unless we were cranky from lack of sleep."

"And are you . . . cranky?"

"We are a mite cranky now, are not we, Ortwine?" she asked Gregory. "But perhaps if we were permitted to sleep for a few hours in one of your most sumptuous guest rooms, our constitutions would be restored, and we would come down the stairs beaming like the lux effluvium at noon."

"Of course, mademoiselle, a room could be prepared for a fee."

"Do you really think for a fee? A fee would make us crankier."

At that moment, several Thusser officers came in. They announced that there was a division moving through, and that they were going to billet themselves at the inn for the day. They had some work to do. The officers demanded rooms. The rest of the men and women would be setting up in the stables.

Gregory was terrified. He prayed that the battery for his costume would hold. He did not want to be unmasked in the midst of their enemy. He sat on the barstool, facing the wall.

The innkeeper excused himself and made some quick arrangements. When he returned, his smile was more sly. He stood across the bar from Gwynyfer. She was eager to get a place for them to hide until this division went past. She asked in a very low voice whether the room for her and her brother was ready.

"You are interested still in a sumptuous room?"

"We are. We would not like to be cranky as we travel on. As I've said, we become very violent when cranky."

"Do you know, mademoiselle, now that I hear you speak more, I become even more interested in your magical and thaumaturgical education. Your accent is undeniably that of a Norumbegan noblewoman. Perhaps you were taught wizardry by some slavish tutor, seized from the City of Gargoyles in times of old?"

"You've touched the matter with a needle."

"Of course, it would be impossible for me to give shelter to any Norumbegan, however blessed with golden kroners. That would be a crime! And I hope that you are not suggesting that your humble innkeeper is capable of subverting the war aims of our glorious Horde."

"No, indeed." The officers were looking over toward the bar, interested in the murmured conversation. Gwynyfer smiled. "Why don't we quit this chitchat? Never mind the lodgings. We'll just be on our way."

"Will you, now?"

"We've already presumed too much on your kindness."

"I thought you were positively desperate for a room. A sumptuous room. I would be more than happy to rent it out to you for a week."

"We have no need of a room for a week. Regardless, we would be gone in a few hours."

"I rent it by the week. If you choose to leave in a few hours, that's your affair. You pay by the week. I should be sorry to see so interesting a specimen travel on without giving me a chance for more delightful conversation — as

161

I say, I am indubitably a 'people person' — but oh well, there it is! Of course, if mademoiselle wishes to leave immediately, I can understand that. And let me say, sometimes it is as interesting to discuss the character of one's guests with other guests — idle speculation, robust anecdote — as it is to observe the guests oneself. Who knows what fascinating insights and conjectures those officers over there, for example, might suggest, if I were to chat with them about two Thusser youths with Norumbegan gold and Norumbegan accents, traveling with their thoughts shielded from inquiry? If you were to leave, I could spend a happy hour discussing the question of your identity with Lieutenant What's-His-Name, musing and tale-spinning. That would make for a very lively forenoon!"

Gwynyfer scowled. "We'd like the room for the week, please."

"Certainly. That will be seven golden kroners. And for ten kroners in toto, I will show you where the fire escape is, in case, mademoiselle, you should find that your room at any point gets too hot."

Furious, Gwynyfer shoved the money across the counter.

The innkeeper bowed and led them up to their chamber.

✳ ✳ ✳

Gregory sat unhappily on the bed. He'd shut off his disguise. He looked merely human, and small at that.

Gwynyfer threw herself back onto the pillows and groaned. "This is miserable," she said. "How am I supposed to know what a Thusser accent sounds like? I've never heard a real one before. And you have to keep silent. We'll make up an excuse."

"How are we going to find Brian?"

"*Would* you stop fretting over that little waif, G? Oh, look, complimentary toothbrushes. I do call that sumptuous."

Gwynyfer slept for several hours. Gregory could not. He stared out the window. Thusser soldiers were all over the inn, carrying out their military errands. Several of them practiced marching in the walled garden. One walked back and forth on the slate roof, carrying an antenna, then disappeared.

In the early afternoon, there was a rough knock on their door.

"Hello?" called a voice. "Sergeant Bogen of the Horde."

Gwynyfer snapped awake. She pulled herself upright on the pillows and braced herself with her thumb over the toggle switch of her disguise. She called out, "I suppose some people still take note of a 'Do Not Disturb' sign on a doorknob."

"Army business, miss. We understand you and your brother are the owners of the two thombulants in the stable. The three-legged and the five-legged."

"Those are ours."

"We're going to have to requisition them."

Gwynyfer's jaw dropped in indignation. "Do you mean *steal*, sergeant? You are going to *steal* our thombulants?"

"Would you come out and discuss this with us, miss?"

"I certainly will not. One doesn't curtsy and make nice with highway bandits."

The sergeant now took a more pointed tone. "You and your brother: runaways, miss?"

"Is this what the Thusser army spends its days doing? Talking to people through hotel doors?"

"You two are traveling on your own through a war zone. Are you runaways?"

"Our parents died in an unfortunate accident with a blast of demon-fire, after denying us use of the wagon for a high school hop. We're cast away on the shores of an unfriendly world."

"You're going to have to come with us."

At this, Gwynyfer gestured frantically to Gregory to open the window and prepare to slip out via the fire escape. She sounded calm, however, as she said, "We'll do no such thing. And you cannot have our thombulants or our wagon. We want to go abroad to make our fortune. It will be a heart-stirring, weepy tale of pluck, courage, rags to riches . . ." She barely knew what she was saying anymore. Gregory was outside the window. He clicked on his disguise just in case, and motioned that Gwynyfer should follow.

She turned on her disguise, too, and backed toward the window. It was time to make their getaway. "Tell me," she said, "what do you need our thombs for?"

"Transport."

She rolled her eyes. "Tell me at greater length what you need our thombs for. This is no time to be brief."

164

She stepped over the windowsill. The sergeant was saying something. She couldn't hear what. She yelled back into the room, "I see. Go on."

And then she and Gregory sneaked down the fire escape.

"What now?" he whispered.

"Blamed if I know," Gwynyfer muttered. "We can't cross the marsh. And we can't get our wagon. The stables are full of soldiers."

They were on the ground. They flattened themselves against the stone wall of the inn. They crept along the side, ducking beneath the windows.

They went through the archway that led into the yard.

And there was a woman in a long Thusser military coat waiting for them.

"The runaways," she said. "I'm Lieutenant Kunhild. You're coming with us."

✳ ✳ ✳

On an endless causeway across an endless flat marsh, a division of the Thusser army marched. They were accompanied by wagons, jeeps, carts, and an old bus with its windows painted black. In the middle of them marched Gwynyfer and Gregory, not speaking a word to each other, anxious about when the batteries of their disguises were going to wear out.

Lieutenant Kunhild had originally suggested that they should be taken prisoner until their parents could be found and their circumstances examined. Gwynyfer had quickly offered that they were active members of their local Young Horde troop, and would be invaluable to the war effort if they were not thrown in chains. The lieutenant asked them what badges they'd gotten.

Gwynyfer had said, "Pardon?"

"What badges? You know. Camping. Arts and crafts. Incendomancy. Torture."

"Oh, almost all of them. Ortwine here didn't get his murder badge because he felt pity at the last moment, but if you starve him long enough, I'm sure he'll become as vicious as the best of us."

So there they were, marching as junior members of the armed forces. Gregory reflected that this was not exactly where he wanted to be: fighting for the race that was seeking to enslave all of New England and other worlds beside. He didn't know what to do. He had no idea how they were going to find Brian. He just felt tired. Unnaturally weary. He wanted to go to sleep and never wake up.

They marched for hours. They were headed, apparently, for Pflundt, which had become the headquarters of the Thusser invasion.

They marched along with other Thusser children. It appeared that the adult soldiers brought their kids along on military campaigns to teach them the lessons of strength and plunder. There were ten Young Horde scouts traveling with the division — six boys and four girls. They didn't talk much, but Gregory got a sense of a few of them: Aelfward, a big, wide-shouldered, handsome boy who took an immediate interest in Gwynyfer and showed it by

166

ignoring her completely; and Druce, a pudgy, short, silent kid who kept muttering spells to himself and clearly was thinking creepy thoughts about girls.

Occasionally the kids in the troop talked to each other. Usually it was six-foot-two Aelfward teasing one of the girls, to show Gregory and Gwynyfer that he was the leader of this little pack, and that Gwynyfer would do well to pay attention to him.

Gwynyfer whispered, "He hasn't even asked my name."

Gregory pointed out, "You'd lie to him anyway."

"He doesn't know that."

Gregory looked at her jealously.

"Look, Ortwine," said Gwynyfer, stroking his cheek quickly, "don't get all boiled in your skivvies. These are just kids. Just Thusser."

They walked silently, hoping that their disguises would hold out.

Late in the afternoon, they saw part of the surface of the slime ripple. Something was floating on top of the marsh like the skin on hot milk. It gathered itself.

A soldier yelled, "Thordath!" It appeared to be a warning.

The skin raised itself up; underneath it was a body with wheeling legs and feelers. It screamed at them and flapped its gooey canopy.

The soldiers scrambled and fired at the monster. It swarmed toward them. They fired another round of blue bolts. Now it yelped in pain and sank into the murk.

Gregory was glad, suddenly, that he and Gwynyfer hadn't been on the causeway alone.

* * *

They made camp on an island covered with low stone houses.

Gwynyfer tromped over to the wagon to demand her pavilion.

"Hello," she said to the adjutant, who was checking things off on a clipboard. "I'd like my silk pavilion, please."

"Yours?" he said.

"Yes. Big, spacious, with cloth-of-gold rugs? It was in this wagon?"

He smiled icily. "The one with the coat of arms of a Norumbegan noble family on the side?"

Gwynyfer bit her lip and nodded. "Yes. Spoils of war. Not mine originally, of course. Ah well, never mind. Never you mind! Not necessary. Thanks awfully. Thanks."

So she and Gregory set up the tent that had been his and Brian's.

As they sat by a campfire, eating baked beans out of a can, some of the soldiers began pointing at the sky.

Gregory looked up. There was Tars Tarkas, wheeling in the air, looking down at their tent.

Several of the soldiers had grabbed their guns. "First one to get it," one said, "I'll give a bag of hot dogs."

The soldiers laughed and aimed at the little bacterium. Aelfward grabbed a rifle, eager to impress the men around him. Tars didn't understand the danger and bobbed closer, looking friendly and hopeful.

A bolt of blue light ripped past him.

The bacterium opened his beak in shock. He hissed and wheeled, uncertain what to do.

More shots were fired.

"NO!" said Gregory. "NO, DON'T!"

The boy rushed to the side of the sharpshooters and pulled the nozzle of a rifle down. "Stop it!"

"What's your problem?" the soldier grunted.

"Don't bother with it! It's just a bacterium!"

Aelfward looked at him in astonishment. "So what does it matter?"

Gregory didn't know. He looked anxiously toward the sky. Tars Tarkas lingered there, uncertain of whether Gregory and Gwynyfer were friendly or not. Gregory willed the thing to fly away — fly away as quickly as it could.

"It never did anything to you," he said.

"And it never will," Aelfward pointed out, "if we kill it."

They turned back to the sky.

The bacterium was gone.

✳   ✳   ✳

They arrived at a town on the edge of the marsh of slime. Here, the troops were transferred to a train that would take them directly to Pflundt.

Lieutenant Kunhild called them into the first-class car, which she had taken over as her HQ. "We haven't been able to locate any word of your parents. Yours is becoming a fascinating case. Where did you say your parents were when you finished them off?"

169

"They were in the City of Gargoyles. Underneath Mount Norumbega. Back on Earth. We had a new condominium."

"It's a shame that no one there has been declared dead."

"That *is* a tearing shame. But it does prove how wonderfully clever my brother and I are at murder-craft. We're rare ones for hiding a corpse."

"Your accent is fascinating. And why doesn't your brother speak?"

"Ortwine doesn't have anything to say. He has no conversation. Bandying words with this fellow is like dribbling an aluminium ball." She squeezed Gregory's arm affectionately.

"And how did you get from the City of Gargoyles to the Great Body?"

"Do you know, Lieutenant, asking too many questions of children is unmannerly?"

"And I think it's unmannerly for children to shield their thoughts. One might even say suspicious."

"Always pointing the finger at the runaways themselves! When, in fact, society is to blame."

The lieutenant sighed, ran her hand across her forehead, and blinked her black, irisless eyes. "Make yourself useful. We're putting you in charge of feeding the animals." She gestured to a man who stood at attention. "Private, show them where the feed is kept."

They spent the next half an hour going back and forth between feed bins and cages of branfs who squawked with displeasure. Then there were red sheep that had to be fed. Then white cows with red ears.

170

Finally, they were given a dish of pellets and told to drop it off in the livestock car at the end of the train.

The door to the livestock car was guarded by several men with rifles.

"Watch out," said one of the guards. "It bites."

"What?"

"The animal."

Gregory and Gwynyfer exchanged a look.

The guards slid the door open.

Gregory walked cautiously in.

There was almost no light. There was straw all over the floor.

And there, in chains, was Brian.

EIGHTEEN

Gregory and Gwynyfer stared in shock. Brian was streaked with grime. There were tracks in the mud on his face from tears. One of the lenses of his glasses was cracked. He wore no shoes. His T-shirt was stained with sweat and wavering tide lines of salt.

Gregory was about to ask what had happened. But then he realized that the door was still open. The guards outside would be able to hear him.

Brian's face lit up in a smile, which he quickly hid. He assumed his friends were there to save him. He thought that this was his big moment to escape.

They put down the bowl of food pellets and the bowl of water in front of him.

They could feel the guards' eyes on their back.

Brian's face fell. They could see him panic.

They turned and walked out of the car.

The door slammed shut behind them.

"Mean little bugger," said the guard. "They're trying

to soften him up and weaken him so he can be absorbed in Pflundt."

"He's a chubby little affair," said Gwynyfer. "He could probably house a family of four."

The guard smiled. He said, "Well, as the saying goes, girly, it's not what's down here" (patting his belly) "it's what's up here" (tapping his head). "And he's a fertile one. A lot of thought-power that'll be nice for someone to sink their feet into."

Gregory was openmouthed and had nothing to say. He wildly spun plans to save Brian, but couldn't think of anything that would work, since they were surrounded. He was terrified of ending up in the same spot. He and Gwynyfer made their way back along the rattling train cars to their seats. He threw himself down and grabbed his own knees. The other Young Horde kids were sitting on duffel bags, drinking syrup and playing throwing games with ornate knives.

Gregory wanted to talk with Gwynyfer. Her eyes warned him to keep silent.

The kids kept throwing their knives closer and closer to Gregory's shoulder. They didn't say anything about it. They clearly wanted to see how the new boy reacted. The blades twanged and stuck out of the woodwork. He slid his eyes to the side and saw a throwing knife had barely missed his headrest.

Facing the other way, Aelfward asked Gwynyfer, "What's your friend's name?" He threw his knife. It stuck into the wall opposite them.

"Brother," she said.

Aelfward was irked. He strolled across the compartment like someone with too much leg muscle to move easily and pulled his knife out of the wall. With a sudden jerk, he hurled it back over his shoulder. It stuck in the floor, right between Gregory's feet.

Aelfward adjusted his question. "What's your brother's name?"

"Ortwine."

"Ortwine." Aelfward snickered. He sat next to Gregory. Gregory could smell the kid's cologne. Aelfward said, "What are your games, Ortwine?"

Gregory had no idea what to answer. He knew soccer was probably not the right answer. So he stared straight ahead without speaking.

A pretty girl called Ianogunde, with full lips, black eyes, and careless hair, leaned back on her elbows and said something that sounded like a line of poetry.

"He gone deep in Lefling, no torn tarp for him."

Aelfward replied, "As kings of Durrenward fathom, no dope can hold the earl with claws."

And another boy said, "No sneaky maw, neither. As Fanchrott at piers. (No fathom, but league.)"

Everyone laughed. It was a game — clearly — a game for which Gregory and Gwynyfer did not know the rules, or the meaning, or any of the references to Thusser history that a Young Horde scout might make.

Kids kept saying things about Gilliard's silly harness and Mudwad weighing bread on scales, and all of it

174

seemed to make fun of Gregory, but in ways he couldn't understand.

Aelfward, next to Gregory, leaned close to the boy's fake ear as if he were about to kiss him. He whispered, "What's your pain, Ortwine? No tongue to talk?"

Everyone waited.

"No one worth talking to," said Gregory. Then he got up and strode away down the train corridor.

✳ ✳ ✳

"Good job," whispered Gwynyfer when she found him.

"Good job at what?" Gregory protested. "What are we going to do about Brian?"

"Nothing, G. This isn't the moment. We're surrounded by Thusser."

"We have to do something."

"We have to blend in. That's the only way we'll save Bri-Bri. You're doing marvelously. I think walking out like that was a success. The cad Aelfward was surprised. That little spud Druce laughed a lot, and I think the girls appreciated your savoir faire."

"My what?"

"You looked like you knew what you were doing. Who you were insulting."

"What was that game they were playing?"

"Who knows? Thusser. It was some game having to do with poetry and rearranging Thusser runes." She put her arm through his. "You did just the right thing by keeping your yap shut." He couldn't believe she was actually praising him. He felt a glow. He said, "You think so? You really think I did a good job?"

"Aelfward hates you. That's a marvelous achievement for just one day." She smiled tenderly at him. And then she leaned forward, closed her black eyes, and kissed him on the cheek.

He put his hand to the spot. "Aw, shucks," he said, with his old humor. "You know," he said, "I forgot how good it feels to put someone down."

"It's a warm feeling down here, isn't it, G?"

"That's right. I've forgotten what I'm all about. Jokes. Being a jerk."

"G," said Gwynyfer, "this is a perfect opportunity. I'm glad to be here with you."

They watched the landscape go by for a while. Derricks and mine works passed like bony carcasses rotting on the stomach's bleak plain.

✳   ✳   ✳

When Gregory rejoined the other Young Horde troopers later that evening, there was more respect for him since Aelfward clearly hated him. Gregory felt good again. His only wish was that he knew how to work with Thusser poetry or throw knives so he could go on the attack. His cheek still tingled where Gwynyfer had kissed it. He wanted that to happen again.

The train rolled on through the night. By keeping silent and listening, Gwynyfer and Gregory started

176

to get a sense of what was happening behind Thusser lines.

The invasion was clearly stretching Thusser resources. Even though there was very little armed resistance to the Horde, they weren't yet in the Great Body in large numbers. They had to come via Earth. The only portal to Earth was the one Gregory, Brian, and Kalgrash had come through — and it stood in the middle of the slimy swamps of Three-Gut. All the Thusser who came through had to be ferried across that endless wasteland of muck. And then their magic was severely reduced because they didn't have enough imprisoned minds yet in which to anchor themselves in this world. They felt exposed, being only in their bodies. They were gathering prisoners in Pflundt so they could feed on their psychic energy. Brian, clearly, was one of these.

They were also rounding up submarines. As Brian, Gregory, and Gwynyfer had heard, the Thusser planned on attacking the Dry Heart and New Norumbega within days. They couldn't do that, however, without subs.

To make matters more complicated for them, the Great Body was showing signs of life. Several hearts had started beating. This made navigation difficult. The lux effluvium was growing warmer and brighter. There had been quakes in the Esophageal Cantons that suggested something might be on the way down the gullet and into the guts.

On the other hand, the Thusser found the citizens of Norumbega remarkably easy to conquer — lazy, disorganized, and self-satisfied.

177

Gregory had heard the fungal priests of Blavage speculate on why the Great Body was coming back to life: They had believed that strife was thought, and so now that there was warfare in the Great Body, it lived again.

The Thusser had a different theory. They, like the fungal priests, believed that the Great Body thrived on the thoughts of those who lived within it. But they thought it had lain as if dead for more than a century not because it lacked strife — but because the Norumbegans, who'd made their home in its guts and lungs and hearts, were now too lost, too apathetic, and too stupid to perk it into life. They were its brain, and its brain was apparently empty.

✳ ✳ ✳

Aelfward took up four seats when he slept. No one was going to argue with him. His boots were big and his coat was twisted around him, and it looked like it would be tough to move him.

Gregory and Gwynyfer were crouching against a wall, trying to drop off. A cold draft trickled along the floor of the train car. "If you were a hero and a gentleman," said Gwynyfer, "I'd be sleeping on those seats, not him."

Gregory looked at her slyly. Then he looked at the sleeping Thusser boy. He got up and stepped carefully across the slumbering bodies of the other Young Horde scouts. He gently shook Aelfward. "Aelfward. Aelfward! Hey, Aelfy."

The eyes opened.

Gregory jerked his thumb at the door. "Lieutenant wants to talk to you."

"Kunhild? What for?"

"She won't tell me. She says it has to do with your skills." Gregory crouched down and whispered, "Four cars that way, third door along. Here, I'll show you."

Aelfward got up and fixed his hair in the window's reflection. He walked along in front of Gregory.

"What's your accent?" asked Aelfward. "Where are you from?"

"Our parents had a place on Earth. The new condos in the City of Gargoyles. Before they erupted."

"The condos?"

"Our parents."

Aelfward stopped and looked into Gregory's black eyes. "How'd they go?"

"Demon-fire. On a Friday." He pointed at a door. "Lieutenant's in there."

Aelfward opened the door. It was a feed closet filled with buckets of branf pellets and hay. Gregory shoved him in, slammed the door, and dropped the bolt in place.

With Aelfward thumping angrily behind him and calling him incomprehensible names through the door, he walked back to the Young Horde car.

He told Gwynyfer, "My lady, your bench awaits you." He gestured graciously at the four empty seats. Gwynyfer smiled at him, pulled herself up on his hand, and went to settle herself more comfortably.

Gregory watched her sleep. Her hands were curled up

179

under her sugar-perfect face. He fell asleep counting the risings and fallings of her breath.

✳ ✳ ✳

Gwynyfer woke up with the unpleasant, squat Druce breathing on her hair. When she opened her eyes, his eyes loomed in hers. He snorted deeply, drawing something in his nose back into his throat. Then he swallowed hard. He blinked several times in surprise. He did not expect her to be awake.

"There's games," he said. "Aelfward's torturing the animal."

"What animal?"

"The human animal. We're going to watch. You could come with me special."

Gwynyfer got up quickly, keeping as far away from Druce as possible. The other kids were gone. Gregory was still sleeping.

"Ortwine!" Gwynyfer shouted. "Ortwine!" She went over and shook Gregory's arm. "They're torturing that awful human thing."

Gregory scrambled up and looked around, shocked. He and Gwynyfer ran for the livestock car with Druce creeping along behind them.

Gregory was terrified. From what they could get out of Druce — who was trying to impress Gwynyfer — Gregory pieced together what had happened: A soldier had found Aelfward in the feed closet. Aelfward was too proud to say that he had been trapped in with the pellets

180

as a prank. Instead, he'd said he was ordered to feed the animals and the door had locked behind him by accident. So then he had to go around feeding the animals.

When he got to the human animal, he asked the guards if he could play some games.

They said sure. No blood, no foul.

Gregory was frantic at what might be happening to Brian. But he was also sick with worry for himself. He knew everyone was watching Gwynyfer and him. He knew that their disguises wouldn't last forever. At any moment the illusion would fade and — *whoomf* — they'd have whites in their eyes. Their black coats would be gone. And Gregory's ears would be stumpy and round.

Gregory and Gwynyfer ran along the rumbling passage.

The door to Brian's cell was open. Inside, the Young Horde scouts were gathered in a circle, grinning.

Aelfward had hung Brian up by the chains on his wrists. Brian's arms were stretched straight in the air. His toes barely, barely touched the floor. He swayed from side to side with the juddering of the train. He had to dance on his tiptoes to keep his arms from pulling out of their sockets. He let out sharp, agonized breaths as he veered left and right and fought to keep standing.

Aelfward reached over and poked Brian in the stomach. Brian's leg jerked up, his whole weight hit his shoulder, and he screamed in pain.

Aelfward reached out a wiggly finger toward Brian's underarm. In a high baby voice, he sang, "Chuck the chick, chuck the chick, chuck the chick under the chin."

181

He started to tickle Brian. The boy flinched, made a noise, could barely breathe.

Gregory charged into the circle.

"Hey!" said Gregory. "Stop!"

Aelfward did stop. He stared at Gregory. The others stared, too.

Gregory stood unsteadily. The train rocked beneath him. He had no idea what to say now. No Thusser he'd ever met would have protected Brian. If Gregory wasn't careful, he'd be up in chains, too. With Gwynyfer hanging by his side.

"What's your game?" asked Aelfward. He was clearly still miffed about being shoved into the feed closet. He stepped forward and pushed Gregory back by the collar. "Why're you sour, Ortwine?" Aelfward looked from the one human to the other. "Not a friend of yours, is he?"

Gregory could feel everyone staring.

He had no plan. He just had to get Brian down from there. The train hit a curve in the tracks, and Brian was racked in agony. He danced on tiptoes like the Sugar Plum Fairy in razor-blade slippers. He hissed with pain *en pointe*.

Gregory said, "There are other games the animal can play."

Aelfward glared.

Gregory went over and tried to pull the chains off the hook high on the wall. He couldn't reach. He was several inches shorter than Aelfward.

"The proud orphan needs help," said Aelfward, reaching up and unhooking Brian.

182

The dark-haired human boy collapsed against the wall, sobbing with deep breaths. He rubbed his shoulders and his red, bleeding wrists. He clearly didn't want everyone staring at him. He turned away and hid his face.

"The animal seems to believe the games are over," said Aelfward. "Up your sleeve is . . . ?"

Gregory froze. He didn't have any ideas. Anything had to be better, though, than Brian having his arms slowly torn out of their sockets.

"Dancing," he said. "We'll dance."

He took Gwynyfer by the hand and led her to Brian as if offering her at a fancy ball. "Music!" he said.

Two of the Young Horde began to thump out a rhythm against the train on the wall of the car. A girl began to sing an old Thusser waltz.

"Dance, fatty!" crowed Gregory, as evilly as he could. He pushed Brian and Gwynyfer together. "Dance, human filth!"

Brian, unbelieving, looked at Gregory.

Gregory couldn't wink at him. He couldn't give him any sign. The other scouts and the guards were all watching him. He couldn't explain to Brian that he had to be cruel to save all three of them.

Brian began to stagger in Gwynyfer's arms.

"Dance, you little vermin!" Gregory called. He saw Brian's white, horrified face float by. Gwynyfer threw back her head and howled with laughter.

Gregory hoped she was just putting on a show.

This was fine, Gregory thought. *Humiliating, but not dangerous. Brian will thank me.* Brian and Gwynyfer moved in dizzy circles.

And then someone threw the first knife.

Gregory swore to himself. He should have thought of that. Of course that's what they thought he meant by dancing. They were throwing knives at Brian's feet.

The human boy's feet were bare and covered in mud. They were still marked by red slices from an attack a few weeks before in the Imperial palace. Despite spells, the scars weren't fully healed.

Now a blade struck right next to the foot. Another thwapped into the wood of the floor.

Gwynyfer pushed Brian away in surprise. She didn't want her feet hurt.

Druce snuck forward and plucked up the knives, returned them to their owners.

The kids took turns throwing as Brian scampered as if drunken. He tried to keep his feet in the air as much as possible. He was exhausted. He bounced against the wall.

The train jolted on the tracks.

A woman's voice rang out. "What's the pleasure here?" Lieutenant Kunhild stood in the door, watching them play.

One of the boys reported, "Tormenting the animal, ma'am."

Gregory never thought he'd be relieved to hear the lieutenant's voice, but now he welcomed the interruption. The dance stopped. The singing stopped. One boy was still banging out a rhythm on the wall, but otherwise, everyone just stood and waited. The train rattled.

The lieutenant walked into the cell. "No interruption. Sing." The girl picked up her waltz. Kunhild bade them, "Dance. Make merry."

Brian sagged against the wall, his mouth open, sweating.

Then the girl Ianogunde swayed forward in rhythm, took Brian's hands, and began to spin him. "He's repulsive!" she said, in time to the music. "He's sticky! He's wet! My pet person!" She laughed with her deep, cherry lips.

She held Brian's hand and spun him out as if they were doing a routine. When her arm was fully extended and Brian tottered at the greatest distance, Aelfward threw his knife, and this time it sliced Brian's heel.

The whole crowd, Lieutenant Kunhild included, burst into cheers. Brian fell to one knee. Ianogunde rushed to him and lifted him up. She kept him waltzing, pressing his soaking head to her shoulder as if they were in love. She rolled her eyes in mock ecstasy.

Everyone whooped and clapped.

Gregory and Gwynyfer did not. Gwynyfer stood without moving near the door, her face tipped up. Gregory just looked desperate.

The dance went on. Brian had trouble walking now. He was limping. His right foot left a smudge of blood at each step.

"We regret the blood," said the lieutenant. "No more blood." She turned to Gregory. "The babe Ortwine. I like a young man to enjoy my regiment. A young man needs to collect those memories of camaraderie and shenanigans in foreign parts to treasure in later years, when the bones are soft and things are quiet in the nest. But you, little Ortwine, you don't seem to have the requisite spirit of kick-up-your-heels. You look positively ill at ease. Green around the gills. What ails you, Ortwine? I wonder whether you know our human animal here. I wonder whether you met when you were on Earth. You're not old friends, are you?"

Gregory looked at Brian, forced to canter in circles with Ianogunde screeching, "You're foul! Foul!" in the boy's ear. He looked at the smirk on Lieutenant Kunhild's face.

And then he spluttered, "No! No, I don't know him!"

There was no reason, Gregory thought quickly to himself, to get locked up, too. They couldn't help Brian escape if they were also —

"So play along," the lieutenant ordered. "Unless you know him."

She pointed. Brian sagged in Ianogunde's arms.

Everyone was watching Gregory. He went into the middle of the circle.

One two three, *one* two three, *one* two three went the music. Two kids were singing now in ugly harmony. *One* two three. *One* two three. *One* two three.

And Gregory began to kick his friend's wounded foot in time. *Kick* two three. *Kick* two three. *Kick* two three.

Brian said, "Please . . . Please . . ."

And the lieutenant smiled as Gregory kicked his friend's wounds, and the dance went on and on and on.

NINETEEN

When Lord Rafe "Chigger" Dainsplint stopped to think about how the old game of life was treating him, he felt heavyish in his gut. Things were not going swimmingly for his lordship.

Lord Dainsplint came from one of the most ancient and noble Norumbegan families — a family that had often worn the purple and ermine of high, even royal, office. He owned much of the city of New Norumbega and many other organs beside. He had grown up surrounded by luxuries, drinking pearls dissolved in wine, eating peacock with the tail fanned. Two weeks earlier, he had almost been elected as Regent and Prime Minister of the Empire of the Innards, and perhaps would have now been the most powerful man in the Great Body if people hadn't taken unkindly to his murder of his chum Gugs — which he thought was rather blinking dank of them, considering that no one ever could really stomach Gugs when the chap was alive (often rattled on a bit; brayed, even; a terribly slow card player).

Two weeks before, Lord Dainsplint had considered himself almost at the top of the Norumbegan hill of beans: views from the palace windows, long afternoons spent playing polo on droneback, plenty of champagne and orange juice for breakfast.

So now it was somewhat difficult to face up to the fact that he was sitting in a grubby undershirt, prisoner in a fortress carved entirely from snot.

Encrusting one wall of Three-Gut's vast stomach was a huge flow of phlegm, dried over centuries into great swaths and columns and ripples. The mannequins had chiseled their way into this shimmering cliff and had created a towering fortress with battlements and turrets of mucus hard as stone.

Exactly how Lord Dainsplint had ended up imprisoned in Pflundt was a complicated tale, and one he didn't really want to think about too hard. He had been exiled from New Norumbega, of course, after shooting Gugs (people can be so dashed particular), and he'd wandered the Dry Heart at first, uncertain where to go. Eventually, he'd paid for passage on a sub headed to the Splenetic Wastes, where he owned a hunting estate. He had the thought that if he got bored of shooting beasties in the crannies and crevices of the wild, he could always pop over to the monastery next door — St. Diancecht's — where he knew a monk who was an expert in herbal poisons. If he ever wanted to go back into politics, it seemed necessary to have a few undetectable and fast-acting toxins in his kit bag.

He hadn't gotten far. In midstream, the passenger submarine he was on had been surrounded by Thusser vessels and threatened with destruction. The Thusser boarded and steered the thing to Pflundt.

And now here sat Lord Dainsplint, favored son of a glorious family, in a prison yard, eating plain rice off a scrap of brown paper bag.

The only good news was that he had been chosen to act as social manager for the Norumbegan prison population. He arranged the distribution of food and the sleeping arrangements and the amateur theatricals. He made sure that the noble families in prison got a separate table and didn't have to eat with the peasantry. He had met some splendid people in the last week — some very solid eggs — and it was always a bit of a shame when they were dragged off to some location where their wills were broken through torture, their minds were laid bare, and they were melded into the walls, alive but corpse-like, psychically fed upon by Thusser, young and old.

Dainsplint looked up from his meal of rice and saw that the gates to the prison yard were opening. Several guards came in, and between them, a new set of prisoners.

Dainsplint stood. It was time for him to do his duty. He handed his rice to a grubby child who stood near him — "Finish it off, Rufus. You look a sight too spindly." — and marched over to greet the new prisoners.

"Hell-o, all. The Honorable Rafe 'Chigger' Dainsplint greets you and all that rot. Welcome to General Herla's

Holding Tank. Delightful you could come. We hope you'll enjoy your time here, et cetera. I'll be showing you to your cots and the mess hall and whatnot. And you are . . . ?"

A man with a white walrus mustache bowed. "The Honorable Osbert Darvish, Baronet of Twilly Steadham, greets the Honorable Lord Dainsplint, and expresses his delight to be imprisoned and tortured with such a worthy peer, who surely will extend protection for his lowly servant."

"Yes . . . I wouldn't get too giddy about my protection, old tripe. A day or two and you'll be feathering some Thusser mum's nest." To himself, Dainsplint thought: *A mere baronet! Puffing around as if he expected the red carpet and servants in livery! Poor old duffer looks like he'll break easily.* "And you are?" he asked the next couple, who presented tear-stained faces.

He was dealing with a family of eight — the horrific Drastlumpkins, most of them wailing for toys — when suddenly he spied a familiar face.

A grubby human boy with broken glasses.

His accuser. The boy who'd unmasked him as a murderer.

Brian Thatz.

Lord Rafe "Chigger" Dainsplint smiled. "Well met, Brian, old flick. It's so delightful to see you. Let me throw an arm around those husky shoulders." Dainsplint squeezed Brian as hard as he could. The bones popped a bit.

Dainsplint's grin was wolflike. "Well, my son, aren't we going to have times?"

✳ ✳ ✳

Gwynyfer and Gregory's Young Horde troop were housed in an old machine shop in the lower reaches of Pflundt. Someone had laid out cheap air mattresses for them, and a Norumbegan lady had been webbed to the wall, her eyes and mouth gaping wide, lost in dreams, so that they'd be able to feed on her energy. She wore an oversize sweater and leggings. She still had on large earrings, which swayed when, occasionally, her head bobbed.

She made Gregory and Gwynyfer nervous.

Gregory said they had to get out on the streets and start checking out the city. "Two things we need to find," he whispered to Gwynyfer. "Where Brian is and where the capsule is."

"Oh, lordy, the capsule. The capsule! You people and the capsule!"

"Look, Gwynyfer, it's the only one-step way to beat the Thusser. The Norumbegans can't stop them. The mannequins can't stop them, obviously. So we have to get the Rules Keepers to stop them."

Gwynyfer gritted her teeth and nodded. They left the machine shop and walked through the streets.

The last time Gregory had been to Pflundt, it had been full of mannequin life. There had been vendors and hawkers in alleys, mechanical families dressed in proper suits promenading on the avenues. If the mannequins were given their independence, this would become the capital of their nation.

Now the gray, cobbled streets were nearly empty. There were signs of the violent assault that had taken the city. Huge chunks of wall were blasted to pieces, and neighborhoods were empty shells. The mannequins who remained now served the Thusser, carrying armaments through the streets or even carrying Thusser dignitaries on platforms. For the first time in more than two centuries, the mannequins had to cook again. In public squares, they made cauldrons of stew for their Thusser overlords. In kitchens, mechanical men sliced up alien vegetables. Butchers hacked at the haunches of many-legged beasts.

There were not enough Thusser to fill the city. Most of the shops and houses were closed up.

"You know what's happening, don't you, while we stroll around?" said Gwynyfer.

"What?"

"The other chaps are poking holes in our inflatable mattresses."

"Look," said Gregory. "That must be the prison down there."

They stood on a bridge partway up the cliff. Down the slope, through a tangle of rooftops and chimneys, was a gray, paved yard that had been outfitted with razor wire on its walls and giant Thusser runes of warning or condemnation. Norumbegans were sitting on the cobblestones in the courtyard, trapped and dejected.

"I'll bet Brian is in there," said Gregory.

"Perhaps," said Gwynyfer, shrugging. "If he hasn't already been brain-sucked."

Gregory surveyed the place, leaning over the railing. He mused, "There has to be some way in there."

"Oh? We could give ourselves up. We'd be in there in seconds."

"Don't be a bore," said Gregory, trying to speak a language she understood. "It will involve disguises." He wagged his eyebrows.

"I do love disguises. Too bad these ones are going to quit soon, and leave us with the Thusser crawling all over us like ants swarming on a turkey carcass."

"We can't replace the batteries?"

"On garbagy little items like these? No. They're throwaway."

After they'd looked around the city, they stopped at a café where they ate awful little Thusser cakes and drank tea grown in the moist hillocks of Axial Organ #6 ("Slumber-Bear Daydreams" — decaffeinated). Gregory urged Gwynyfer to talk to some of the other Young Horde scouts who were slouching at nearby tables, reading magazines. He was too worried that his accent and his ignorance would give him away.

She inserted herself into a group, pulling up a chair and sitting on it backward. Gregory watched the way she touched her hair or boys' arms and the way she laughed. He wanted her to laugh that way with him.

Finally, he watched as two boys, eager to show off, stood up and displayed their scars for her.

When they left the café, Gwynyfer had a lot of news.

"Something big is happening tomorrow. They don't know what . . . the Norumbegan prisoners are being kept in that walled yard we saw, but only until they're needed in a Thusser dwelling or encampment. That's as we expected. . . . None of the fellows there have seen three mechanical giants carrying a capsule of any kind. Stupid move on my part — they were a mite startled by the question. Did seem too awfully specific. . . . As for the mannequins: The ones who've been taken prisoner are allowed to run down — no one winds them up — and they're stowed in a factory down at the foot of the cliff until they're needed. They're not being used for psychic fertilizer because the structure of their thought is too alien. That factory's the best guess as to where three mechanical giants might be stowed. All clear?"

"Let's go to the factory," said Gregory, and when she rolled her eyes, he grabbed her wrist and started running. He knew that speed and recklessness would please her.

They pelted down through the gray, empty streets. They galloped down winding staircases that crisscrossed the cliff, and arrived at the factory breathing heavily and laughing.

It was made of dull brick. Some of the high windows were broken from nearby explosions. There were two Thusser guards standing by the front doors with long rifles and bayonets.

Gregory said, "Should we claim our troop wants a personal tour?"

"No. That's nuts."

Gregory nodded. "Then we're just going to have to find a way to break in," he concluded.

They went back to their barracks for dinner and a poor night's sleep on their punctured and deflated beds.

✳ ✳ ✳

Brian did not have a good night's sleep. Lord Dainsplint had arranged for Brian to share a cell with him. This was just so his lordship could torment him.

Brian came back from dinner to discover Lord Dainsplint standing next to their bunk bed.

"D'you know," said Lord Dainsplint, "it is a tragedy that the terrors and mishaps of childhood so often plague us in later years. I, for example, was once locked in a haunted butler's pantry overnight. The expressions and expostulations of the dead quite unsettled me. To this day, I find that being in an enclosed space — such as a small cell — often prompts in me a horrible spate of bed-wetting."

Brian looked at his lordship. He said, "That's my bed you're wetting."

Dainsplint looked down. "So it is, old fish. So it is." He walked off to look out into the prison yard through the bars of the door.

So Brian had not slept in a bed. He'd slept on the cold, hard floor. And every time he finally got to sleep, Dainsplint had started singing a menacing old folk song about wringing the neck of a fat little goose.

Brian was exhausted. His nerves had been attacked magically. His foot was festering with an untended wound. He had a fever. He had hardly eaten for days. His best friend had betrayed him, somehow — Brian couldn't tell exactly what was going on there. He kept hoping that the door would burst open and Gregory would be there, dressed as a . . .

But even Brian couldn't work out a scheme to escape.

All night, he lay kinked up in the corner of the cell, and he felt the goopy Great Body all around him. He felt the cold, hollow passages and squelching systems unfurling in all directions through all of time and space — and he himself was nothing but a little wad of organs and quivering muscles in the midst of those vaster innards. There was no wall behind which something was dry and safe. There was nothing but ruin and corrupted body: his own weary and scratched flesh, his empty stomach, and then the stomach around him, the Volutes wound around it like clouds around a globe — and the unimaginable distances that had to be traveled before the dead, dry heart could be found again.

✳ ✳ ✳

There was one scrap of good news. As Brian ate the flatbread that was shoved through a slot in the morning, he heard a clatter at the window. A dragony face looked in.

"Eew!" cried Lord Dainsplint. "An heraldic bacterium! Filthy!"

Brian ran over to Tars Tarkas and petted his nose through the bars on the window. He said, "That's funny, coming from someone who wets other people's beds."

Brian tore off a small piece of bread and fed the bacterium. "He followed me all the way from the Volutes. He's a *good boy*. Occasionally, I saw him, but he could never get to me. Once, these soldiers all fired at him."

"Pity they don't train true marksmen anymore."

Brian crooned, "How are you doing, boy? Huh? How are you doing?"

The animal made a weird, cute noise and licked the boy's hand. He tried to force his way into the cell. His shoulders didn't fit. He made frustrated little whimpers and scratched at the bars with the first couple of sets of claws.

Tars couldn't get in, and Brian couldn't get out. They stared at each other through the window. Tars's eyes were deep and green, and seemed to know everything Brian thought and felt. The creature leaned down and licked Brian's knuckle again — then turned with a flick of the tail and flew off toward the crags of dry sputum.

✳   ✳   ✳

Early that morning, on an empty street of row houses, Thusser in top hats knelt, polishing long Alpine horns.

Gregory and Gwynyfer were eating breakfast when the horns sounded.

All over the city, on balconies and towers and bridges, Thusser wearing bright red sashes blasted out one long, urgent note. One horn took it up, then another, then another, then another. The sound rebounded across the frozen cataract of snot and echoed in the swamps.

Immediately, there was activity. Thusser soldiers turned out of houses where they'd been sleeping. They rushed into formation in the city squares.

Word passed from mouth to mouth: General Herla, commander of the Thusser forces in the Great Body, had finally ordered the submarine assault on New Norumbega. It was time at last. The waiting was over. Regiments were on the march to the valves. In two hours, the subs were going to set off into their various circulatory systems, all of them converging on the Dry Heart.

A sergeant came by to tell the Young Horde scouts that they weren't going anywhere. They were going to help staff the fortress while the army fought this last, great battle.

No one thought it would take long.

"What I've heard is that New Norumbega has no walls," said Aelfward. "The army'll be back in a day and a half."

The kids were tremendously excited. They left their breakfasts half eaten and ran for the overpasses where they could watch the soldiers marching toward their subs. The Thusser did not cheer, but they made a strange rasping noise in their throats. The soldiers turned and smiled.

Giant elevators deep within the fortress dropped the soldiers down through the thick layers of the stomach. They crawled into subs of all descriptions: from a few military subs left from the Mannequin Resistance to merchant ships that had been outfitted with guns and torpedoes.

One by one, the subs arrived, docked, were filled, and set themselves loose.

The engine screws started to turn. The flux was filled with muck kicked up from all the commotion.

The Thusser subaquatic force set out for the Dry Heart.

✳ ✳ ✳

Meanwhile, Gregory and Gwynyfer ran down toward the factory where the disabled mannequins were stored.

"This is exactly the right time to break in," said Gregory. "No one's paying attention."

"Topping," said Gwynyfer, playing leapfrog with a bollard.

They slowed down and fell silent when they reached the factory's grim, soot-streaked walls.

There was only one guard out front.

"Okay," said Gregory. "It will be amazing if the Umpire is in there. We'll just wind the three guys up, go inside the capsule, and start figuring out the controls."

"Yes?"

"Yeah. Just think: Single-handedly, we'll be saving New Norumbega. Can you imagine how angry the Thusser will be when they do all this trumpet *BLAH, BLAH!* and all their subs leave, and then they hear that the Rules Keepers are kicking their butts on Earth? Give me five, lady! Give me five!"

"Noise."

"You're right." Gregory led them back along an alley. "Okay. You go and talk to the guard. Distract him. I'm going to climb into one of the broken windows. Give me a hand up."

"How will you get out?"

"Problem for later."

Gregory tested his shoe against the brick. Gwynyfer came to his side, and just when he thought she was going to lock her hands together to give him a hand, she pulled him to her and kissed him on the mouth.

Gregory breathed in sharply with surprise. He smelled the scent of her. He felt how soft her lips were and how strong her arms were.

Then it was over, and she'd woven her fingers into a basket for him to step on.

He leaped up, pushing off against her hands. He grabbed the brick sill of the window. He struggled upward. When he'd pulled his legs up, he gave her a thumbs-up.

Gwynyfer sauntered around front. She walked over to the single guard.

"Hi-ho. You must be one sorry soldier, stuck here when everyone else is off to paint the town red. I call that a too pitiful predicament. Where the blood and glory?"

Meanwhile, Gregory found himself crouching above what looked like a crammed waxworks museum. Hundreds of mannequin citizens stood motionless, uncranked, in whatever pose they'd struck before they'd wound down and dropped off.

He surveyed the crowd. No giants. No obvious capsule. He'd have to search more thoroughly.

He sidled over and grabbed on to a heating pipe that ran up beside the window. The paint flaked off in his hands. He shimmied down to the floor.

He made his way through the silent, eerie storeroom of persons. Hands were caught mid-gesture. Mouths were making words. Eyes stared at him. He had to duck to squeeze under arms.

Nothing. He saw butlers, maids, pilots, a string quartet. No giants. He pushed open some large swinging doors and discovered an even larger gallery of motionless mechanicals. He climbed up an iron staircase to a walkway where he could see all of the mannequins at once. He passed a set of actresses frozen in poses as witches. Or maybe, he considered, they were actual witches.

And then he saw motion.

Just to his right.

He froze.

Nothing moved.

There was no sound. Two vast storerooms of people stood silently.

Gregory slowly turned his head.

Past a couple of newspaper reporters, there was another window.

It was his own reflection that had startled him.

He let out his breath. *Idiot*, he thought, shaking his head at himself.

But then he really panicked.

He pushed toward the window, pressing at his face.

There were no rings around his eyes. He was not wearing a long, black coat. His ears were human. His disguise was gone. The batteries had died.

And if his batteries had died, then Gwynyfer . . .

✳ ✳ ✳

Gwynyfer chatted happily with the guard. She had told him the usual story about having bumped off her parents on Earth. Then the conversation lagged, so they talked about downhill skiing.

Gwynyfer was saying, "In fact, that is the one thing that is happy-making about moving to Earth. The skiing. You may have done psionic skiing in the Tenebron, floating and flying and what not, but do you know, have you ever tried *substance*? I mean a mountain, a physical mountain, and snow? It's terribly exciting. They have mountains there on Earth. In a place called New Hampshire. And you use gravity. It is too, too thrilling."

For some reason, as she made this speech, the Thusser guard looked at her with surprise, then suspicion, and finally amusement.

Gwynyfer decided the best thing for it was just to push on. "You know, when we rule all of the Great Body, there's also skiing here. Sludgier than on Earth, but still. Yes? . . . Long live the Horde and all?"

A band of soldiers was walking past. The guard whistled between his fingers and called them over.

"Friends?" said Gwynyfer. "How too delightful."

She was surrounded by soldiers. They looked her up and down.

"While a girl always appreciates the glances of a crowd," said Gwynyfer, "you do know it's not polite to gawk? Perhaps I'll just skip along."

"Mademoiselle," said one of the officers, "we were just judging a lady of quality. You're of a radiance not often seen in these war-torn, gastric wastelands. We'd like to serve as your escort up the hill."

Gwynyfer didn't like the sound of this. She smiled prettily at them. "Why, though your offer recalls an age of chivalry long past, and while I deeply appreciate it, I regret I'm not headed up the hill."

"Mademoiselle, you'll find that exercise livens up your limbs and promotes circulation. And we offer you perhaps the last exercise you'll enjoy for a while."

"I call that a little ominous, officer."

"Accept my apology for any undertone of hostility or brutish command. Of course I would not wish to cast a shadow over your last day, mademoiselle."

"My *last* day? Why my last . . . ?"

Then she looked down.

There was a ghost of a dark coat fudging the air around her jacket sleeves. And, she imagined, her eyes probably showed through the costume as it faded.

Her disguise was gone. She was a Norumbegan surrounded by Thusser soldiers in the center of a fortress ruled by the Horde.

"Perhaps," she said with a sigh, "I do fancy a brisk walk up the cliffs."

It was clear to Gregory that the capsule and its bearers were nowhere in the ranks of the deactivated mannequins. A thousand things could have happened to it. It might never have reached Pflundt. It might still be toiling across the goopy wastes. It might have come to Pflundt and left. And worst, it might have been discovered already by the Thusser and destroyed.

Gregory started to thread his way back to the window he'd come into. He hoped he could make it back up the pipe and out.

The front doors to the building, several rooms away, slammed open.

Gregory froze. He backed away into the shadows, intertwining himself with mannequin businessmen. Someone could be looking for him. If Gwynyfer was caught, they might have suspected there was someone sneaking around in the building.

A single pair of footsteps was coming up a flight of stairs.

Gregory ducked and made his way toward the wall.

The door to the room Gregory was in burst open.

Gregory kept close to the floor. He froze.

He stayed that way, caught in the room of immobile bodies which all stood like the exhibits of bears and badgers and moose at a natural history museum.

For a long time, he stood still. He admired how smart he was.

Then his muscles began to hurt. His back twinged. He was in a weird position.

He didn't hear any other sound in the room. No more footsteps.

Gradually, so slowly it felt like not moving at all, he lifted up his head.

There was a tide of faces around him. Some had their mouths open. Some had their eyes closed.

Over near the door he'd heard bang open was a young man facing his way and a young woman facing the other way.

Gregory froze again and tried to see if the young man moved. He couldn't remember if the guy had been there when he came in. A mustache. A bowler hat. He would remember a bowler hat.

The light fell through the broad windows and floated like old, brown times through the air.

Gregory stared at the man's face. The man stared back at him.

But it was the woman who raised her arm — the arm of a Thusser soldier — and released a stream of thick yellow gas right toward him from the nozzle of a gun.

Gregory caught her eye in the reflection of the window. She'd been watching. He'd moved too soon.

The gas roiled across the hall, passing over the heads of the frozen mannequins.

The soldier waded through the crowd toward him. She wore a mask over her nose and mouth.

Gregory bolted toward the pipe he'd climbed down.

He grabbed hold of it and started pulling himself up. He kept slipping. She was getting closer. The cloud was almost around him.

It hit. His eyes burned. He had to close them. He couldn't hold on to the pipe. He fell backward, choking.

He hit the floor and rolled, gagging, fighting for breath.

TWENTY

They sat in a row in the prison yard: Gregory Stoffle, Gwynyfer Gwarnmore, Brian Thatz, and Rafe "Chigger" Dainsplint. Their hands were by their sides. They stared at the cobblestones.

Overhead, the lux effluvium burned a bright, hot white.

All four of them were dressed in shapeless gray clothes. They sweated from the heat beating down on them.

Tars Tarkas lay beside the four of them with all six of his short little legs sticking out to the sides and his tail trailing through the dust. His tongue stuck out of his beak and he panted. The afternoon seemed endless.

Gwynyfer said, "I call this a pretty kettle of fish."

Dainsplint daubed at his wet forehead with the hem of his smock. He said, "I do so love to see friends reunited. Stirs the old heart, hm?"

Gregory and Brian looked at each other. The last time they'd seen each other Gregory had been kicking Brian's bleeding ankles while Brian limped in circles with a cackling Thusser beauty queen.

Whenever Brian looked at Gregory's face, he could not help remembering the jolts of pain at every third step: *kick* two three, *kick* two three. When Gregory looked at Brian, he felt ashamed, and then he felt angry, because he had only been trying to help, and Brian obviously didn't understand. Brian closed his eyes and dropped his head.

Across the stone yard, children chased moths.

✳   ✳   ✳

A huge fleet of submarines chugged through the veins. The walls vibrated as they passed by, their propellers spinning. Swimming things sank or scurried.

A balloon with many eyes and a single flipper watched them burble past. When the coast was clear, it began to swim quickly and purposefully away.

✳   ✳   ✳

Kalgrash the troll and the Earl of Munderplast — the gloomy, old Prime Minister of the Empire of the Innards — sat perched on a broken slab of concrete, taking tea.

"Shan't end well," grumbled Munderplast in a voice that sounded like a sad, bored prisoner speaking from a dungeon several rooms away. He looked out over the mess of the city and said in his weird, medieval mutter, "Your walls . . . your walls, with strength and mickle might

208

up-builded . . . We of the Court cannot help but notice that they do not enclose our palace."

Kalgrash corrected him. "The remains of your palace."

"No reason to be unkind. We are all of us remains, dear troll. Vehicles of decay."

"We said we'd protect the Norumbegan people. And we will. But we couldn't protect the whole city. So we chose part. Not the palace. Anyone who wants to can flee behind the walls."

"Aye. And your other ventures? What of your computers, dredged out of the wreckage? Any messages, any missives sent from yon other sphere?"

"No. Not a peep. We have them set up and they're on, but there's nothing happening. There's no one to talk to us."

"Oh, dear troll. *I* will talk to you." The old man patted the troll's claw. For a moment, they sat companionably, looking out at the ruins. Munderplast asked politely, "Does our beloved Empress — may the gods smile always upon her — does our beloved Empress still persist in trying to kill or to magnetize you?"

"Yup, yup, yup," said the troll, eating shortbread. "Last night she tried to have a pallet of bricks dropped on me. But accidentally, the rope didn't break. Day before that, it was a metal-eating virus in my cot."

"You escaped, I wot?"

"I came back late. By the time I got there, it had eaten the bed."

The Earl of Munderplast shook his head. "One fears for the politician who can't carry out a simple assassination.

209

Utter incompetence . . . Still, I suppose, better for you this way: living . . . in as much as living is occasionally superior to deathly oblivion." The earl sipped his tea. "Occasionally," he repeated. "Very occasionally."

A boy came leaping and jumping over the gravel pits toward them. "Sirs!" he yelled. "Sirs! The Thusser are on the move! General Malark sent me! The Thusser are on the move!"

The kid reached their side. He wore the jacket of an Imperial herald. He was out of breath from scampering over the ruins of the palace.

Munderplast asked, "What news, child?"

"There's a mechanical spy down the flux veins. It saw the Thusser fleet. Stolen subs — a whole heap of them on their way up here. General Malark says twelve hours away."

Munderplast stood. He tossed his old china teacup and saucer off to the side. They cracked on the rocks.

"Alas and alack and 'To arms,'" said the earl. "Things are about to get worse."

❋　❋　❋

Gregory and Brian stood in line for brown rice. It was the first time they'd been alone since Gregory was shoved through the doors of the prison.

Brian said, "Sometimes there's a little pork fat, too. Or something like pork."

Gregory nodded. They stood for a while longer. The line wasn't moving very fast.

The rice was cooked in a big metal half-barrel over a pile of embers. The air smelled like burning oil and hot steel.

Gregory said, "I'm sorry. You get it . . . I mean . . . that I had to? . . . Kick you?"

Brian just stared at him. He didn't know what to say. Of course he got that.

Gregory continued, "If I didn't kick you while you danced, Gwynyfer and I would have been captured. They already suspected us. Because of our accents and because the disguises shielded our thoughts."

Brian nodded.

Gregory said, "And also, if Gwynyfer hadn't started dancing with you, that kid Aelfward would have kept you hanging up in those chains." He shook his head. "That was terrible. That was awful. I hated seeing you like that."

Brian nodded again. "I know you did."

"So there's nothing else I could have done. You know?"

"I know."

Gregory stuck out his hand. "So . . . shake? Friends?"

"Friends," said Brian. He shook Gregory's hand.

But he didn't know whether they would ever truly be friends again.

✳　✳　✳

Just as trumpets had sounded above the walls of Pflundt down in Three-Gut, now sirens wailed on the walls of New Norumbega. Citizens crawled out of their huts dragging plastic bags filled with possessions, rushing for the neighborhoods the mannequins had fortified.

Kalgrash and the general sat in the clanksiege, perched on top of the crude new walls. The troll had to be at General Malark's side to tell him what was real and what were simply the illusions of Norumbegan glamour.

"What a mess," muttered the general, watching the crowds of elfin Norumbegans inside and outside the walls. There were brawls down below, and people were running around without point, ignoring the orders of mannequin soldiers. Some people were trying to drag their most expensive pieces of furniture along with them to safety — things their parents had brought hundreds of years before from Earth. Others were looting empty shops and smashing windows, kicking down the doors of apartment buildings to see what was left to steal.

Soon the Thusser would be mooring their submarines at valves surrounding the capital. They'd be crawling out of the ground. They'd be forming ranks in the desert, just as the mannequins themselves had done three weeks before.

Kalgrash and General Malark watched the Empress and her Court borne along on chairs carried by servingmen. She and her servants made their way heavily down hillocks of trash. The Empress cooled herself with a fan.

The troll and the general watched as, in the distance, out in the bright plains, mannequin marines headed off to their vessels to do battle with the oncoming Thusser fleet.

"Good men," said the general. "Good women. But they can't win."

"What do you mean?" Kalgrash asked, horrified.

"According to the mechanized spies floating in the blood, our subs are outnumbered. Wildly. Only hope is that the Thusser haven't had time to bring enough weapons through from Earth."

A jolt ran through the landscape. For one startling moment, the clanksiege teetered. The general swore and banged at the controls. The machine regained its footing. Down on the ground, piles of garbage slid and shifted.

"Another heartbeat," said the general. He shook his head. Down below, in a tent, geologists and mathematicians were hard at work, trying to figure out when each pulse was coming and which way it would push the flux or the lux effluvium.

Now another skirmish had broken out near the new gates. Lord Attleborough-Stoughton, the railroad baron, and Lord Gwarnmore, Duke of the Globular Colon, had started a movement called Equal Walls, Equal Citizens. They objected to the fact that some people's houses and businesses were protected, while others weren't. They were mainly interested in this because the walls would do nothing to protect their own property: the railroads and various neighborhoods at the edge of the city. So they shot off guns and threatened to shoot anyone fleeing into the safety of the walls. They wanted to force the mannequins to protect the whole city, rather than just one part.

"They're crazy," said Kalgrash. "Nuts, nuts, nuts."

213

The general nodded. "We have to decide when to take them both down. Gwarnmore and Attleborough-Stoughton. May they live long and may their fields be fertile."

"The Thusser will be here in just a few hours. We can't have people outside the walls."

"It's a mess," the general repeated. "Living, breathing creatures — they're always a mess. Never trust them, troll. We have to love them. We have to serve them. But don't trust them."

The ground jolted again. Another heart; another heartbeat.

Below, three men in bowlers were in a fistfight over a box of stolen ice cream.

TWENTY-ONE

In the prisoner-of-war camp in Pflundt, the Norumbegans felt safe for the moment. With so many of the Thusser gone, there were no longer the daily visits from overlords looking for victims to attach to Thusser houses. For a few days, at least, families could rest easily that they would not be hypnotized and stuck to a wall.

So they lolled against the walls of their prison, staring into space.

Brian, Gregory, Gwynyfer, and Lord Dainsplint sat in a cell with their arms crossed.

Gwynyfer said, "It smells horrid in here."

Dainsplint said, "Brian had an accident in his bunk. Nervous little blighter."

Brian said, "No. *You* had an accident in my bunk."

"If you can't learn to control yourself like one of the big boys . . . if you insist on needing special pants . . ."

They fell silent for a while. Then Brian said, "I wonder where the Umpire is right now. I wonder how close we are, sitting here."

Gregory said, "We looked for it."

Brian was excited. "You did?"

"Yeah," said Gregory. "No dice. We thought it might be down at this factory in the lower town where they're holding all the windup people. They've let most of the mannequins run down."

"They'd have to," said Dainsplint. "The mannequins were built to serve Norumbega. They'd give their lives to fight the Thusser, if given half a chance." He said grimly, "Pity we lost the secret of constructing the mannequin soul when we lost everything else. We could have built a real army again. Protected the homestead, the hearth, and the happy glade."

Brian asked, "How could you just lose the secret?"

"Because we hadn't done it for centuries. We left it to mannequin manufacturers. I mean, manufacturers who not only *made* mannequins but *were* mannequins themselves. We didn't want to have to work. By the club of the Dagda, a *job* . . . getting a *job* . . . what a thing." He sighed. "So we left it all to the manns themselves. That and everything else. Then came the flight from Old Norumbega, and here we were, many of us dead in the Season of Meals, and the manns all abandoned us like the lazy, willful little tick-tocks they are, and — that was it! We could make drones with simple brains, but gone was the day of the mann with a spring in his step as well as in his knee joint. Gone was the day of the mann with the dahlia in his buttonhole and the poem in his soul. After a while, the little cads concealed the secret from us. Can you imagine the cheek of it!"

216

"So they could still build an army of mannequins, if they wanted to?" Brian asked.

"Of course! When the bloody things build a new mann, they still stick in brains. Fully working brains. A soul and nickel-and-dime memories and the whole lot. They have a factory town that makes heads somewhere around here. Place that does repairs whenever one of them breaks down. New heads, old heads, young heads, gold heads. The whole bit."

Brian took notice of this. He asked, "They have a factory that builds heads?"

"Indeed. About fifteen or twenty miles from here. Kaputsville. That's what it's called. Kaputsville."

"So," Brian pressed, "all their heads come from there? That's the place where all the heads of the mannequin people come from?"

"Yes. Unless they came over from Old Norumbega."

Brian stood up with a triumphant look in his eye. "That's it!" he said. "That's where the capsule is! The capsule and the giants aren't in Pflundt at all! They were headed this way through the Volutes and the stomach — but they wanted to see *where all the heads of the mannequin people came from*! And it must be that town!"

"Kaputsville?"

"Yeah!" said Brian. "The town where the heads are actually made! The actual heads! That's where they went!"

Gregory laughed. It was a weird laugh, kind of jagged and narrow, but a laugh nonetheless. "I bet you're right," he said. "We were looking in the wrong place."

217

"We've got to get out of here," said Brian. He paced back and forth in the cell. "We've got to get over there. The capsule could just be sitting there. There's time to save New England — and New Norumbega!"

"Indeed?" said Lord Dainsplint. "If only we were free?"

"Yeah," said Brian. He went over and looked out the barred windows.

"Then, old sponge, you might wish to turn your attention to me. Because I've been thinking for the last few days, as I sat here, waiting for the dear Horde to drag me off and cook the old noodle till it's *al dente*. And I believe I have come up with a plan."

✳ ✳ ✳

In the caverns of flux, the vast pirate fleet of Thusser subs thundered toward the Dry Heart. And now they met the mannequin marines for the first time. Out of a branching capillary — a vein only a few hundred feet wide — mannequin ships poured, already firing torpedoes at the oncoming host.

Thusser ships burst open like flower pods, dandelion blasts blooming in the green darkness of the flux. Metal skidded through the blood and buried itself in the walls. Still, the mannequins fired relentlessly.

But the Thusser subs kept on coming. They didn't seem to care that they would be destroyed. They didn't fire back. They just chugged forward.

Then one swerved. And another. And they headed

right into the mannequin fleet. They smashed into mannequin ships. They erupted.

Inside the mannequin subs, mechanical men and women in finned helmets clanked desperately up and down ladders, looking out portholes, dropping torpedoes into their firing tubes and launching them.

Gradually, word went out, commander to captain: The Thusser didn't have weapons; they were were using their subs themselves as weapons. They were controlling most of them remotely. They didn't care if they lost them. In fact, losing them was the plan. They plowed them into the hides of mannequin gunboats.

Explosions rocked the veins. The flux was dark with oil. The mannequin navy was surrounded, then swamped.

There was no way they could protect the Dry Heart.

TWENTY-TWO

At dinner in the prison yard, Lord Dainsplint ran back and forth, making sure that dinner was splotched out on plates without a hitch. This was one of his jobs in the prison, but the Thusser guards noted that he was not usually so enthusiastic about his duties. Typically, he spent most of his time lounging on a bench and making fun of the guards for their accents or their socks.

One of the guards muttered, "Watch him."

Dainsplint ran up underneath them and called up, "Hi-ho! Walerond in the kitchen needs to get another barrel of bug-juice out of the cellar. We're running out. Can we borrow the keys to open the bulkhead door?"

The guards were used to this. One of them silently tossed him down the ring of keys.

"Spiffing," he said, catching them in midair.

They watched carefully as he ran over to the bulkhead door and unlocked it. One guard lowered the muzzle of his rifle. One wrong move, and they'd shoot his lordship in the back.

But Dainsplint just did what he often did: unlocked the bulkhead for the cook's assistant. Nothing unusual about that.

From a distance, at least.

As Dainsplint stood, hands behind his back, waiting by the bulkhead, he held a thick piece of cooked fat in his hand and rubbed it against the keys. He slopped them all over with grease.

The cook's assistant reappeared on a ramp, trundling a barrel of juice in front of him. The guards watched Dainsplint slam the doors shut and lock them.

As he jogged back over, he jostled the ring of keys against the fat.

When he got back to the guard tower, he yelled, "Alley-oop!" and tossed the keys back upward.

A guard caught them. "Eh!" he said. "They're all sticky!"

"Sorry!" said Dainsplint.

And crouching in the doorway of their cell, Gregory said to Brian, "Step one complete."

✳ ✳ ✳

Nighttime in the prison of Pflundt.

All the prisoners were locked up in their cells. A single guard sat drowsily in the tower. High above the city of phlegm, the lux effluvium glowed a dull blue-black.

Tars Tarkas was sleeping curled up by the bars of Brian's cell door.

Brian crept over to the door and whispered through it, "Hey! Tars! Hey there, boy!"

The bacterium looked up, blinking.

Brian held up a wad of cloth that had been torn off a sheet, balled up, and rubbed in fat. "Hey, Tars! Fetch!" Brian threw the ball of cloth.

It didn't go too far. It unfurled partway and dropped. But the bacterium was overjoyed. He scampered on his six legs to seize the thing. He charged back to Brian and presented the loose end through the bars of the door. For a little bit, Brian played tug-of-war with the dragony creature. Tars reared his first set of legs in the air and shook his monstrous little head back and forth. He pulled and pulled.

Finally, he released it so Brian would throw it again.

Dainsplint watched carefully as Brian played with his bacterium.

Brian threw the lard-covered ball of cloth farther the second time. And even farther the third time. "Go get it, boy!"

The fourth time, he held it up while Tars danced impatiently in front of him. He feinted — pretended to throw it — pretended again — and this time, clenched it in his fist while making a show of hurling it out into the yard.

Tars didn't notice the cloth hadn't left Brian's hand. He charged out into the center of the empty yard.

"Fetch!" Brian whispered.

Finding nothing, Tars started to sniff around. He disturbed a flock of pigeons, which flew away. He paddled his wings and rose off the ground.

Brian watched anxiously as Tars clearly smelled the same fat smeared on something in the guard tower. The bacterium hovered closer.

The guard in the tower stared bored over the walls, out at the city arrayed up and down the cliff of snot. The streets were dark. Most of the citizens were shut off.

Beside him on the table were the keys to all the doors in the compound on a single ring.

A small, dragony head poked up next to them. A long, snakey tongue licked sideways out of a shiny, beaky snout. It licked the fat smeared on the metal. It tickled at the keys and wrapped itself around their ring.

Slowly, the bacterium pulled the keys toward him.

The guard closed his eyes and settled into sleep.

There was a faint rattle as the keys reached the edge of the table.

The guard woke up and reached out to feel what was there.

He grabbed the key ring and slid it back to the center of the table.

He shifted in his seat and closed his eyes.

Underneath the table, the clever bacterium waited. Tars Tarkas waited for ten minutes. Then slowly, carefully, he snaked out his tongue again and began dragging the keys toward him.

Gently, he lifted them off the table.

When he had them in his mouth, he flew to Brian.

"Good boy!" Brian whispered. He reached out to take the keys from his prancing accomplice. He grabbed a couple and pulled the key ring out of Tars's mouth.

Tars tugged back.

Time for tug-of-war!

"No," said Brian. "Leave it! Leave the keys! Tars! Come on, boy!"

Tars pulled them away triumphantly and scampered back and forth in front of the cell. The keys dangled from his beak, rattling.

"No! Come on! Come on, boy!"

Lord Dainsplint let out a moan. "Little blighter. What blunt instruments am I given for my work!"

Tars presented the keys to Brian then jerked them away, his tail twitching in fun and pride.

"Tars! Please! Come on!"

The guard's chair scraped back in the tower. The guard stood up and bellowed, "What's all that, Cell Twenty-three?"

He looked down from his tower. There was the human boy playing with his wretched bacterium. "Stop it, or you'll lose your arms. And all privileges connected thereunto."

Brian waved timidly. With his other hand, he held the keys in a clump. They were still clamped in Tars's beak.

The guard turned away and sat down.

Brian backed away from the door. Tars's head clanged through the bars.

Brian whispered, "Trade." He held out the strip of greasy cloth. Tars snapped at it, and Brian pulled the key

224

ring away. Tars sat down to give the cloth a good lick and eat it.

Maybe five minutes had gone by when Brian reached around and unlocked his own door. He and Dainsplint slipped out.

They made their way two cells along. Tars bounded by Brian's side, making leaps for the key ring, which he now considered his. Brian unlocked Gwynyfer and Gregory's door.

The four of them flattened themselves against the walls. They walked sideways, in the shadows, to the kitchen door. It was only a space of twenty feet or so — but if the guard looked at them, his Thusser night vision would pick them up perfectly.

Then they were in the dark of the kitchen. The two Norumbegans led the boys past counters and cutting boards. They unlocked the door to the outside world. A stone staircase led down to a back alley.

They were free.

It was time to visit the place where the heads of all the mannequin nation came from.

❋ ❋ ❋

In the veins of flux around the Dry Heart, a severed head drifted through the green. None of the Thusser paid attention to it. There was a lot of wreckage. They did not see that the head was gently rippling with transparent fins.

The head tumbled quietly between Thusser ships. The motionless eyes watched the mannequin host retreating, defeated. Too many of them had been blown up by unmanned Thusser ships plowing into their hulls. The remainder were pulling back to defend the airlocks that led into the heart in the desert around New Norumbega. The Thusser fleet was left on its own.

The head rolled gently past portholes and propellers.

It was a gentleman with a side-part and blue eyes. He had been built to spy. His billowing fins wafted him gently past scenes of Thusser industry.

They were setting something up. Some piece of vast machinery they'd taken from a factory somewhere. Thusser engineers, wearing stolen Norumbegan diving suits, were preparing a huge device for operation.

They did not notice a floating head. There was a lot of flotsam and jetsam in the stream of flux.

The head darted to the side, lurking in the shadows. It watched.

The machine was a drill, the floating head realized. They were going to drill a new passage into the Dry Heart.

It wasn't a blade, the floating head realized. It was a drill. They were going to drill a new passage into the Dry Heart.

The tip of the drill kissed the wall. The divers gave each other the thumbs-up. They began to swim away.

And the drill began to turn. It spun. It was huge.

The head swam off, trying to look as broken and severed as possible. It had news. Important news. Bad news.

The church bells were ringing throughout the city. Noblemen in business suits were standing in the ruins of the palace, dressed in old papier-mâché animal masks, making magic signs with their hands. It was somehow supposed to convince their ancient gods to spare them. Everyone thought they were about to die.

In the streets, Norumbegans were fighting with each other over shelter and donuts.

That was when the quake hit. It was the largest yet. And as the city shook and the walls trembled, the veins of lux effluvium glowed blindingly. New Norumbega was seared with heat.

Shielding their eyes, people ran — screamed — and shanty buildings fell. The light was pitiless.

Then the quake stopped; the lux effluvium faded to its daylight simmer.

Messengers were rushing to General Malark.

"Portion of the wall's down by St. Gwydion Plaza."

"Sir, the shelters on Confectioners Row collapsed."

"Casualty list for the navy, sir."

"Latest word from Barry, sir."

"Barry?" said Kalgrash. "Who's Barry?"

General Malark nodded. "Disembodied head number twelve. He's one of our best men." He asked the messenger, "What's the word?"

"The Thusser are drilling into the Dry Heart, sir. Huge drill."

General Malark winced. He said, "That was probably the quake we just felt. The Great Body's in pain."

"We have word from heads Dennis and Phil, sir, that there are two more drills in other veins. They're all operating at once."

"They're making their own way into the Dry Heart," said the General. "That's how their infantry is going to get in here."

Kalgrash looked out at the shimmering desert. He heard the cries of the terrified citizens all around him. He saw courtiers in wolf masks and deer masks scrambling toward the gates.

"No," he said. "The Thusser aren't going to send in their infantry."

"Eh?"

"They don't care about this city," said Kalgrash. "Dr. Brundish probably told them months ago that it was a dump." He explained to General Malark, "None of our defenses, none of what we've worked on for weeks matters at all. None of it, none of it, none of it. They're not going to invade, General. They're going to flood the Dry Heart, and we're all going to drown."

TWENTY-THREE

Two thombulants carried riders through the dark up the mucoid cliffs. A wandering, narrow road had been carved into the crystalline flow.

Brian and Lord Dainsplint rode one of the thombs; Gwynyfer and Gregory rode the other. Far below them gleamed the lights of Pflundt.

They had stolen the thombulants from a stable near the edge of town. There was no other way to get up to the Kaputsville plateau. Though they were bulky and stupid, the thombulants walked quickly, their flanks swaying from side to side.

They'd been climbing for hours, laboring along the switchbacks. Gwynyfer was asleep, curled uncomfortably sideways on Gregory's chest. He was tired also, but he was too happy to sleep. He was holding on to her, and she was allowing him to. It didn't matter that he was human and she was elfin. She relied on him to stay awake while she slept nestled against him.

Brian, needless to say, didn't feel exactly the same

229

way about Lord Dainsplint, who sat in front of him, making rude comments about the few little villages they passed — grim places with tall chimneys, fixed to the sides of the cliffs.

When the night was almost over, in the darkness before dawn, the cliff shook. At first, Brian thought it was just the thomb, but the quaking kept up, got heavier, and he saw rocks pelting down the slope below them.

"Great Body's shifting," said Lord Dainsplint. He looked up. "The stomach's jolting or whatnot."

There was a hideous slam, and everything jounced. Guinevere wakened and yelped with surprise. The thombulants froze on the path.

Then the motion was over as quickly as it had started. Rocks and stones trickled down the ledges.

Dainsplint grinned. "See? There's life in the old corpse yet."

"Let's go," said Gregory. "We've got to keep going."

Brian said grimly, "They're probably missing us at the prison by now."

Dainsplint explained, "Listen, old pudge, hate to be the bearer of bad tidings, but there's a difference between *missing* you and simply noticing you're gone. Not sure if anyone actually ever *misses* young Brian Thatz. 'Oh, I say, Waxmuth, where's that droopy human number who's always complaining about fairness and Vermont? I really do like to start my day with an earful of simian whinge about freedom and pine trees.'"

Brian kept his mouth shut. One way or another, he wouldn't have to take this much longer.

They kept riding. Murky hours passed. Gwynyfer fell asleep again. Brian wanted to fall asleep, but he felt as if Dainsplint was keeping an eye on him.

They were high up on the cliff of phlegm. Iridescent gleams caught on the huge formations above them.

The veins of lux effluvium grew bright. The air grew warmer.

As dawn spread throughout the stomach, they came within sight of a plateau of heads.

At first, the huge shapes were dark and domed in the sunrise. But then the veins in the sky shone brighter. The blue glow caught on carven features: a massive eye, the bridge of a nose. Brian and Gregory squinted to make out what they were seeing.

It was the town where mechanical brains were made with souls wound on sprockets, and the engineers who had built those brains had carved their shops to advertise their wares. So each shop was itself a giant head: domed scalps and eyes peering out across the void, far across the darkling plains of chyme; full faces some, with noble noses and gentle lips, while others peeked out above the plateau, mischievous and half sunken. There were giant babies with wisps of hair barely sketched on their skulls, gazing into a future that might never come. There was a young woman of beauty; there was a young man who laughed; there was an old woman whose lines spelled out the understanding of pain.

The heads stood immobile on a cliff far, far above the marshes of Three-Gut, motionless in the morning winds.

"We're there," Gregory whispered to Gwynyfer. She

wriggled in his arms and sat up, stretching. He felt her shoulders with his hand.

It was not long before they came across the site of a battle. Clearly the mannequins had fought hard to defend the little town against the Thusser invaders. On a rough rise, there were blast marks and an overturned jeep. A set of mannequins lay, blown apart, on the heath, their gears and clockworks blackened. There were several Thusser graves — pointed mounds of earth with gray, filmy banners rippling out of them in the wind like the tags on chocolate kisses.

The kids and the elfin nobleman slid off their thombulants to search the mannequins for intact heads. The Thusser had smashed all the survivors, however. Lord Dainsplint found a rifle that looked like it was in working order. He slung its strap over his shoulder. Brian and Gregory inspected the Thusser graves.

"Don't touch the banners, kids," said Lord Dainsplint. "They're charged with memories. You'll be flooded."

They boys backed away and mounted their beasts. They galloped up toward the town of heads.

The lux effluvium now shone like it was full day. Gregory said, "Hey — when we were in Three-Gut a few weeks ago, it was never day. It was always kind of dark."

Brian said, "The lux effluvium must be circulating. Because the Great Body is coming back to life. And it's heating up, too. Everything's changing."

"I think it's just corking the Great Body's stirring," said Lord Dainsplint. "And I say, about time, too."

Brian asked, "Aren't you worried that it might, I don't know — move? Or get up? Or cough or swallow or something? And that everything will be wiped out?"

"See, you *are* a gloomy little mite. Whenever there's energy and chaos and change in a system, it's time for someone clever to profit by it. Someone with a biting wit and a sleek, fashionable head of hair. Yes, old boot, I mean myself."

Gregory grinned. He liked Lord Dainsplint, in spite of himself. He wanted to be that way some day himself: the smart, savvy one who figured things out before anyone else. And maybe Gwynyfer — maybe they were married by then? — they could have an apartment in New York where all their furniture was hard and rectangular, or maybe white and spherical, and they'd —

The first shot hit a thombulant. The creature reared up, throwing Gregory and Gwynyfer to the ground. The beast blew out a painful blast of steam.

Cowering on the ground, Gregory looked around for the gunman.

Bolts of light were sailing past.

A sniper. A guard up by the town firing down on them.

Lord Dainsplint had slid off his mount and hid behind it. Brian, meanwhile, couldn't get off, because the animal was panicked, and reared up on its hindmost legs as bolts blasted the rocks around them.

Gregory saw a ditch about ten feet ahead of them. "Come on!" he hissed to Gwynyfer. "Crawl!"

But she shrieked — for she had already been hit.

233

$$* * *$$

The drills around the Dry Heart whirred and rasped, tearing away at its wall. The flux was murky with torn meat, ribbons of muscle cored out of the flesh.

New Norumbega had been rocked by several quakes. People just sat on the heaps that remained. They did not try to save themselves. There was no way to stop what was happening. If the Thusser broke through, everyone would die. The Norumbegans of flesh needed to breathe — and almost all of the mannequins, if soaked for long, would begin to misfire, to malfunction, to short, to seize up, and therefore to die.

The scene in the city was one of absolute chaos. No one bothered to protect anything. Fathers wailed. Mothers gouged at one another for pushing too hard or shoving. Babies screamed. Crazed teens laughed.

Kalgrash sat on top of the wall. His legs stuck out straight. It was the end. General Malark was off trying to guide the navy in one last attack on the Thusser drills.

It wouldn't work. No one thought it would. There were too few ships left.

Kalgrash lay his battle-ax beside him. There was no smiting left to be done. No house under the bridge. No warm afternoons. No cozy winter nights by the fire. No more skating. No more anything.

Kalgrash realized he had only lived a year — and now it was over.

It was so unfair he felt like crying.

Someone was running toward him. A kid. A real Norumbegan dressed as an Imperial page.

"Mr. Kalgrash! Mr. Kalgrash, sir!"

"Yup?"

"The computer! That your guys found! It's started sending messages!"

Kalgrash struggled to his feet. "Huh?"

"It's sending messages!"

Kalgrash grabbed his ax. You never knew when you might need to smite, after all.

"You're kidding," he said.

"No," said the boy. "And it's asking for you by name."

TWENTY-FOUR

The thombulants stampeded back and forth in terror. The sniper still fired down at the group.

Brian couldn't jump off his steed. It was moving too quickly, too violently. He'd get crushed. Tars Tarkas flapped and swirled around his head, growling at the distant gunman.

Gwynyfer was screaming in pain. Her foot was mostly gone. In a ditch, Gregory was pulling off his shirt and wrapping it tightly around her missing toes. It was already red with her blood.

Up in the town, the sniper hid behind a wall. He snarled into a walkie-talkie that he might need reinforcements. He lowered his gun and aimed it at the top of the blond boy's head.

The thombulants galloped in opposite directions.

And as they parted, they revealed Lord Dainsplint standing behind them with the rifle he'd found, pointing it up the hill. He shouted the Cantrip of Activation and it fired.

The sniper flopped backward, dead.

It was a ragged band that finally wandered into Kaputsville. Gregory had no shirt. Lord Dainsplint had the scummy start of a beard. Brian's glasses were cracked, and his feet were bare and sliced up. He hadn't bathed for days and his hair stuck up crazily. Tars Tarkas was crusted with dirt and cranky. Gwynyfer staggered on a bloody, bandaged foot, using a slightly twisted metal signpost as a staff to hold her up. She winced every time she stepped.

No one made any jokes or sly remarks. They walked past the dead guard and into the center of the little town. They were among the giant faces.

The ear-holes radiated black soot, as did the eyes. It was like the heads had thought something so terrible it had blown their brains. There were doorways into the head stores, sometimes on the cheeks, sometimes on the back of the skull, and a few times, replacing the faces. The doors were blasted off. Clearly, there had been explosions inside the skulls.

Chunks of their stone faces spilled across the plateau. The heads were huge and wounded.

Brian and Lord Dainsplint walked into the first face they came to. The empty cranium echoed with their footsteps.

Inside, there was nothing but black walls and a few pieces of furniture, almost burnt beyond recognition.

Dainsplint said, "You think the blinking Ump is here? I'm not sure that anything's left in this town."

He walked back out into the light of the lux effluvium.

237

They went into several of the head-shaped houses. There was nothing but incendiary ruin.

"The Thusser blew everything up," Gregory said. "They destroyed everything."

"I think not," said Lord Dainsplint, squatting on the ground. When he stood up, he held a device in his hand. He said, "I think the mannequins destroyed it. This is a mannequin grenade, unexploded."

"Huh?" said Brian. "Why would the mannequins destroy their own town?"

"Because this is where the manns make and restore their own souls. They didn't want the Thusser Horde to find out how it was done. So they probably held the Thusser off down there for as long as they could — and then they blasted apart their own workshops. Protect the secrets of their trade and whatnot." He frowned and looked around Kaputsville.

Gwynyfer, who was having trouble breathing from the pain of her wound, sat down and leaned her head against the nape of a neck.

Brian said, "That was why the town was only guarded by one Thusser. There's nothing here to guard anymore. It's empty."

"What do we do?" Gregory asked.

No one could answer. They knew that hundreds of miles away, along the great network of veins and arteries, battles were being fought, and even as they stood, looking at the vast, dismal sea of slime thousands of feet below them, people were dying.

They searched the other houses.

There was a lot of twisted metal. There was dirty glass. There were small remains of mannequins who'd been blasted to bits.

Gregory stopped searching to check Gwynyfer's bandages and make sure his shirt was still tied tight on her foot. She was in a lot of pain, and kept grunting.

As he knelt by her and yanked on the sleeves of the shirt, he happened to look up at the dull hills above the town. Something was moving. It looked like a church steeple.

He said, "One sec," to Gwynyfer, then ran over to call Brian and Lord Dainsplint. He found them in an old man's head, inspecting some footprints in the ash. "Something's coming," he said to them.

They went outside.

Coming down from the hills were three mechanical giants. They were blackened with soot. They were heavy and their limbs were thick and their arms would have reached almost to the ground, if they had not been carrying something.

In their arms was a chapel of some kind: a tiny, stone Gothic booth with stained-glass windows only a foot wide, and little buttresses and finials and spires. It had a door in its side. They carried it by its buttresses.

They advanced slowly.

"Whoa," said Gregory.

And Brian said, "So here it is."

The three blackened automatons marched the Umpire Capsule through the village of shattered faces.

✳ ✳ ✳

The giants each faced a different direction. The capsule was raised between them. They stood on the edge of the cliff, looking out across the marshes.

Lord Dainsplint and the three kids faced the giants. Tars was sniffing the capsule.

Behind the giants, somewhere far out in that sea of goop, lay the black portal where, three weeks before, the boys and their troll had entered this world. Brian squinted out at the horizon, but he could not see those faint ruins, that staircase in the air. Since then, they had been gassed, scissored by droids, shot at, pinched, hypnotized, tortured, and, perhaps worst of all, insulted continually by the very people they were trying to help. They had flowed through veins of flux and traveled the wastes of the Dry Heart. They had crawled through the Volutes like yesterday's dinner.

And now, standing before them was the capsule they had sought so long. Its slim stone arches and stained glass glittered in the light of the belly.

Down the slope, several jeeps were making their way up the rough road from Pflundt toward the town of heads. It looked like they were crammed full of Thusser soldiers with guns.

The giants spoke, one word at a time.

"The." — "Thusser." — "Came." — "We." — "Hid."

Then:

"We." — "Believe." — "It." — "Is." — "Time." — "For." — "Interruption."

Brian stepped forward. "Yes. Yes, it is." He didn't know what to do next. He raised his hands like a wizard.

The wind blew through his mossy hair. "Interrupt!" he commanded.

The three giants turned toward him.

"We." — "Cannot."

Gwynyfer, dangling from her signpost crutch, said, "Well, that's a bit of a clunk."

The giants explained, "You." — "Must." — "Enter." — "And." — "Activate." — "The." — "Time." — "Out."

Gregory and Brian rushed over.

"Dibs on the controls!" said Gregory. "I call hitting the button!"

"If there is a button," said Brian. "And not just something you touch and then say the Cantrip of Activation."

Gregory rolled his eyes. "Okay! Now that we're about to finish, could you for once stop pretending that God gave you golden pants just because you know the stupid Cantrip of Activation?"

"I'm just saying that —"

Gregory reached up to the old, iron ring that opened the door to the little gothic capsule. He swung the door open.

He and Brian might have kept squabbling if Lord Dainsplint hadn't interrupted them.

"Hey, old bucks. Dashed sorry to interrupt the interruption, but it ain't going to happen."

The boys stopped and looked at him. He smiled. He said, "If you interrupt the Game — if you call back the Rules Keepers — if they come and blow the bally whistle and sock the Thusser out of Old Norumbega, then all of us — all the citizens of the Empire of the Innards — will head back to our old haunts back on Earth."

"Yeah," said Gregory. "That's the idea. Duh."

"That's *your* idea," said Lord Dainsplint. "But you forget, there are certain noble and gracious people — and I count myself one of them — who own most of the Dry Heart, who own plantations in the spleen, who own mansions in corky old organs that don't even have names. And if everyone flees the Great Body, we, sorry to say, will be spang out of luck. And I, my dear children — I do not like to be out of luck. Luck's a filthy lady, lads, and never let anyone tell you different. Whenever you want to feel lucky, and plucky, and brave, pick up, for example, a grenade."

He held up, in his hand, the unexploded mannequin grenade. He tossed it lightly up into the air and caught it again.

"I helped you come here not so that we could all grasp hands and sing 'Hooray' and snatch victory hot off the griddle. I came here to destroy that bloody capsule once and for all."

"But the Thusser!" Brian protested. "If you destroy the capsule, the Thusser will take over the Great Body and you won't have anything! Not a city, not an empire, not anything!"

"On the contrary, young Thatz. As I said: Whenever there's energy and chaos and change in a system, it's time for someone clever to profit by it. Someone with a biting wit and a sleek, fashionable head of hair. So . . ." He held the grenade above his head. "As much as we've all become close in the last weeks, and as much as it would be right and good and dandy to do the square thing by my little chimp chums, I'm afraid that what I'm going to do instead — is blow you all to hell."

TWENTY-FIVE

Lord Dainsplint hooked his finger through the pull ring of the grenade. He eyed the jeeps that were swerving up the slope toward the plateau of heads. "I need the Thusser to witness your detonation. I shall want them to recognize my excellent qualities as a friend and ally, hm? So hold that pose, blunderkinder."

Gregory looked over the edge of the cliff that was about to be blown apart. It was three or four thousand feet down. Then he looked at the two Norumbegans who stood staring at him a couple bus-lengths away. Suddenly Gregory felt the difference of their species. Their ears seemed more pointed. Their faces seemed even more clever and more uncaring.

"Gwynyfer?" he mewled. "Are you . . . ?"

She just smiled at him.

"She's one of us," said Dainsplint. "Not one of you. She does not have enthusiasms like you people have." He smiled. "Sorry, old thing."

Though Gwynyfer sagged and was wounded — though

243

Lord Dainsplint was grubby and covered in sweat — they stood side by side as confident as if they were in some mirrored hall in a fairy palace.

Then Gwynyfer slammed the Honorable Lord Rafe "Chigger" Dainsplint on the back of the head with her signpost. He didn't even have time to cry out. He fell face forward. He hit the ground and lay there. The grenade was still clutched lightly in his hand.

Gwynyfer said, "He isn't wrong. But a girl can still enjoy the thrilling novelty of knocking someone senseless with a length of metal." She hobbled toward them. "Next time I might —"

Whatever joke she was going to make was cut short by jeeps. There were two of them buzzing between the giant heads, kicking up dust and soot.

The door to the capsule was open. Brian jumped in and Tars flew in after him. Gregory ran out to support Gwynyfer — "Chivalry!" she cheered — and he helped her make the final few steps to the little arched doorway before the bullets began to fly past them.

They slammed the door shut behind them. They heard the blasts of Thusser rifles.

They were squeezed in close. There was hardly room for all of them to stand. The little booth was lit by stained-glass windows. The control panels were made of stone. Norumbegan runes scrolled across every surface.

"There aren't any buttons or switches or anything!" said Gregory in panic.

Brian burbled the Cantrip of Activation loudly. Nothing happened. He tried it again. Nothing.

An amplified Thusser voice from outside demanded, "Leave the capsule. Leave the capsule and you will not be harmed immediately."

Gregory muttered, "I don't suppose they mean, 'Leave the capsule immediately and you will not be harmed.'"

Brian glared at the runes. He was dazzled by the jewel-like light of the windows cast across the crammed little letters. The words were unfamiliar to him, scientific, magical. He saw nothing that could be clicked or flicked or turned on.

They could hear Thusser soldiers running toward them across the gravel.

"How do we turn it on?" said Gwynyfer. "How?"

"I don't know," Brian muttered. "I don't know. . . ."

Outside, two Thusser soldiers hurried over the gravel terrain to the fallen Lord Dainsplint. "You! Hands up!"

His lordship groaned and writhed. "What?" he said. "Is this a dance routine?"

"Hands up!"

They pulled on his hands — "No, not my!" — and the pin flew out of the grenade.

Lord Dainsplint whined in horror, "Now look what you blinking idiots have —!"

And then there was an explosion.

The ledge was blown to bits.

The capsule flew into the air.

The giants fell; the capsule fell; boulders large as houses slid down the face of the precipice.

And inside the capsule, Gwynyfer slammed her hand down on the stone panel.

The capsule stopped falling. There was no motion whatsoever. The light through one white, clear window cut sharply at an angle, as if they'd paused in midtopple.

There was no noise outside. Nothing.

Everything was still.

"What'd you do?" Gregory asked.

Gwynyfer said, "The light from the stained-glass window . . . it's the buttons. I hit the spot of red above the rune for the Cantrip of Activation."

His voice filled with wonder, Brian whispered, "Time-out. A real time-out."

"Huh?" said Gregory.

"Time outside the capsule has stopped or something. Until the Game can be judged by the Umpire."

Light slid across the stone. The design on one stained-glass window was shifting. The window now showed two coats of arms.

A voice said, "You have initiated a time-out. The Capsule of Interruption is a joint venture of the Norumbegan Imperial Synod of Wizards and the Enclave Sorcerous of the Thusser Horde, designed to adjudicate violations of the rules detailed in the Treaty of Pellerine, twelve ninety-seven A.E. You have initiated judgment. The capsule is prepared to call the Rules Keepers, as mutually agreed. False or exaggerated claims will result in forfeiture of one round. Do you wish to continue?"

The kids looked at each other. Then Gregory called out, "Sure."

"Please enter your initiation code for verification."

Gregory and Brian looked at Gwynyfer. She shrugged. Tars Tarkas licked his claws, curled up in the vaulting of the ceiling.

"We don't have any code," said Brian. "But the Rules are being broken. Right now. In a big way."

The machine said, "We will require verification from one of the two parties involved in the treaty. Do you wish us to contact —"

"The Honorable Gwynyfer Gwarnmore, daughter of the Duke of the Globular Colon, greets the Umpire Capsule, and demands that —"

"We will require verification from one of the two parties involved in the treaty. Do you wish us to contact the communications terminals at either the Imperial Court at New Norumbega or the Magister of the Thusser Horde?"

The kids exchanged glances.

"Imperial Court," said Brian. "But I don't think they pay any attention to their computers. I'm not even sure they know where they are."

The machine warned them, "To communicate, we will have to re-enter time."

"See," said Gwynyfer, "right at present, we're rather falling off something of a cliff. So we wonder whether we could avoid hitting bottom. And the dying."

Suddenly, there was sound outside the capsule. Things falling, crashing, wind blowing.

But the capsule was suspended in midair — a chamber in the sky.

Gregory peered out a clear pane of glass. He saw the ground hundreds of feet below.

While Brian and Gwynyfer inspected the control panel, two small wooden panels, painted with the ancient gods of the Thusser and the Norumbegans, swung open. Behind them was a screen.

On it, runic letters in an old, glowing green font said:

```
Connecting with the Communications Center
of the Imperial Court in New Norumbega. . . .
Connecting . . . Connecting . . .
```

Then the screen flashed and the following words appeared:

```
Hello?
   Hello?
   Testing?
   New Norumbega here. Is there anyone out
there?
```

"There's someone on the other end!" Brian exclaimed.

"What do you want me to type?" asked Gwynyfer. She prepared to touch the runes.

The conversation went like this:

```
Hello. This is the Umpire Capsule. The Hon.
Gwynyfer Gwarnmore here with Gregory
Stoffle, Brian Thatz, and some kind of
grub that's hanging on the ceiling. Please
```

```
authorize  the  interruption  of  the  Game
ASAP.


Hello.  Nim  Forsythe  here,  ma'am.  Mannequin
guard,  posted  to  watch  these  machines  for
activity.  I  don't  know  anything  about
authorization.  Please  help  quickly.  The
Thusser  are  drilling  through  the  Dry  Heart.
We  are  about  to  be  drowned.  Please  help.
```

"Spiffing," said Gwynyfer sarcastically.

Brian said, "Tell him to get someone else! Someone from the Court!"

"And who's that?"

```
Go  get  the  Earl  of  Munderplast,  the  Empress,
and  Kalgrash  the  troll.  Tell  them  it's
urgent.
```

And the guard wrote back:

```
Going.  Please  wait.
    Please  help.
```

✳ ✳ ✳

Kalgrash sat down in front of the computer terminal. He could hear beeping and static from the modem that communicated to the capsule. He wriggled his fingers in the air above the keys. "First time typing," he said.

```
hey there htis is kalgrash. i just learned
to read so dont kick my typing.


Kalgrash   this   is   Brian,   Gwynyfer,   and
Gregory.


Sweat to heer from you!


We need you to get the Earl of Munderplast
or the Empress or someone to enter a veri-
fication code to activate the capsule.


earl of m and empress e on their way. let
me go look for them.
```

Kalgrash ducked out of the tent that contained the transplanted computers. He looked around.

Total chaos. Screaming, people throwing bricks, crowds surging through the streets.

He ran up the fire escape of a nearby building. The whole city rocked yet again. The whole heart. The whole Great Body. It flinched.

Far out over the shrugging walls, over the broken roofs, out in the desert, there was a plume of green. It grew like a stalk of grass.

Kalgrash swore.

It was a geyser. It was getting bigger.

The Thusser had broken through.

And now a second one appeared, off toward the Autumn Ventricles. A huge jet of alien blood.

The first fountain still spewed. At its foot was a grow-ing lake of flux.

The end was here.

Kalgrash looked down. Now he saw the Empress and the Earl of Munderplast trying to make their way through the streets toward him.

The troll clambered down the fire escape, his armor clanking on the metal. He ran toward them, hustling people out of the way. "Your Majesty! Your Majesty!" he cried.

Angry noblemen were screaming at the Empress, "Shame! Shame!" — "What can you say, Your Highness?" — "You let this happen!"

As she tromped forward, she yelled back at them, "Oh, dry up! You're the ones who wanted nothing but tea dances! I am protector of my people, and I —"

"Shame!" citizens screamed at her. "Shame!" — "We're trapped now! What do you say to that?" — "Yes, what's your plan, ma'am?" — "Shame! Shame!" — "My kids!" someone sobbed. — "We're all going to die!" — "Curse on you, ma'am! A curse!" — "Shame on the mother of the Emperor bomb!" — and they began hurling pebbles at her.

"You know, my people," said the Empress, shielding her head with an imperious hand, "you're becoming some-what of a thorn in the side."

Kalgrash jumped in front of her, swinging around his battle-ax. "Back!" he shouted. "Or I smite!" He didn't like her, but everyone needed her to get to that com-puter console.

251

"Oh, you," said the Empress. "Thought I'd had you magnetized."

The crowd shouted horrible names at her. They threw pieces of metal.

Kalgrash shielded her — the woman who'd tried to have him killed — and walked with her and the earl toward the tent where the computer waited for them.

Out in the desert, the flesh of the Dry Heart was tearing. The whole plain rattled. Another heartbeat, somewhere else — and the flux swelled up from the ground, the lake of it stretching across the dunes, washing through villages and over tombs.

Kalgrash, the Empress, and the earl stumbled into the communications tent. The crowd screamed for blood outside.

Soon they would get it.

Kalgrash said to the guard, "Nim, go out and keep people away."

The man nodded and darted outside, shouting, "Please be orderly! Please!"

The equipment glowed on the desk.

"Oh, one of those," said the Empress, looking at the computer. "Frightful sort of time to play Pong."

"The code!" Kalgrash shouted. He couldn't control his anger anymore. He took the Empress of the Innards by her shoulders and shook her. "Your Highness! The code! To release the Rules Keepers!"

(A tide swept across the desert. Houses and towers tumbled in its waters.)

The Empress said, "Munders, do you recall the Treaty of Pellerine? Some centuries ago?"

The Earl nodded. "Oh, in the old labyrinth of memory, where so many ancient and noble things be wrought, there, in some neglected corner do I recall —"

Kalgrash dragged the man to the folding chair. "START TYPING!" he said. "START TYPING THE CODE!"

(The tide smashed against the walls. And another wave. And another, throwing up bursts of garbage. Broken concrete plates slid backward as the waves retreated. Electrical poles were engulfed as new waves hit, splattering green spray.)

Concentrating mightily, the Earl of Munderplast — who was not a typer — began pressing buttons one finger at a time. His old, wizened finger picked out one rune after another. Slowly. Slowly.

Another earthquake hit.

This time, half the tent collapsed. Chunks of building thudded into the ground.

The whole Great Body writhed in pain.

The flux broke through the walls. It poured down in great bursts. It sloshed through the streets. People struggled to climb higher, but everything had collapsed.

In the sagging communications tent, plaster dust hung everywhere. Kalgrash saw the old man still hunched over the computer. "Keep typing!" he screamed.

The guard, Nim Forsythe, called in, "Ma'am! Sirs! The flux is in the streets! It's rising!" The Empress gathered her robes in one hand to prepare for the inundation.

"Done!" said the Earl of Munderplast. He hit ENTER. "And sent!"

"Yeah!" said Kalgrash. He felt incredible relief. Help was coming. That's what mattered.

He looked at the screen.

`Signal lost. Please re-enter.`

Then he realized what had happened. Part of some roof, falling onto the other half of the tent, had cut off the antenna. The computer hadn't sent the code off to the capsule.

"Nim!" he shouted. "Get in here! We have to fix this!"

The guard charged back in.

Kalgrash pointed at the end of the antenna wire that poked out of the rubble and the torn green cloth of the tent. He pointed at the other end of the wire, coming out of the back of the computer. It was clear where the falling debris had cut the wire.

"We have to join those two ends together," said Kalgrash. "Don't touch the wire itself — just the insulation. There's like a million volts going through there. Until the flux wipes out the generators."

They each grabbed an end and pulled them toward each other. A few pieces of concrete shifted. The two automatons yanked.

There was no way the severed pieces of wire were going to touch anymore. Three feet of antenna were missing.

"Lackaday, lackaday," groaned the Earl of Munderplast. "We all shall die most dismally."

Then Nim Forsythe, mannequin guard, looked at Kalgrash and at the Empress of the Innards. They heard the tide of flux thundering into the city. They heard the screaming of the people. Nim Forsythe climbed on top of the desk.

And he reached down and grabbed the other wire from Kalgrash's hand.

He touched the two ends of the exposed wire with his bare thumbs.

Immediately, he jolted. The current was running through him. He had become part of the antenna. His mannequin brain scrambled — blew.

"Hit return again!" yelled Kalgrash to the old man at the keyboard. "Send again! We only have a second until —"

The medieval Earl of Munderplast pressed ENTER. The code was sent.

And Nim Forsythe, who had given his life to save the empire, collapsed, all memory blanked, all energy sapped, all workings fused.

✳ ✳ ✳

General Herla, commander of the Thusser Horde in the Great Body, smiled as he watched the drills bore into the Dry Heart. He stood on a submarine observation deck surrounded by officers and by the idiot corpses of Norumbegans who'd half sunk into the walls.

"They're finished," said one of the officers. "I'm sure most of the Norumbegans in the Dry Heart are already dead."

General Herla said, "Give it another few minutes. Then we can pull the drills out and send a sub in to explore the wreckage."

Without thinking, he leaned on the face of an old, dreaming Norumbegan man who'd been absorbed into the pipes and wires of the sub. With his elbow on the man's gaping mouth and broken jaw, he stared out at the hole in the heart.

✳   ✳   ✳

As the signal code from the communications tent flew through organs and between worlds, the tide of flux swept almost as quickly over houses and tombs and towers. Families on rooftops screamed. People at the base of the new city walls splashed toward steps. Kalgrash stomped toward a high mound of rubble with the Earl of Munderplast over his shoulder. He let forth a long warrior's yell, but there was no one to smite and no one to hear.

Parents lost hold of children. Buildings shifted and collapsed. Huge sparks flared where the electrical generators of the city died. Hands reached out. Mouths gasped for breath.

Soon, there would be no place left to stand.

New Norumbaga sank beneath the waves.

TWENTY-SIX

Three mechanical giants stood, holding a gothic capsule on top of a mountain. It was a sunny day late in the summer. There was a sky, which was blue, and far to the east lay the Presidential Range of New Hampshire: Washington, Jefferson, Adams. Though the sun was warm, a brisk breeze blew.

The arched door of the capsule popped open. Three kids and a slithering little six-legged dragon stepped out. The blond boy dropped and kissed the ground. "Earth, I love you! I love you, Earth!" Gregory exclaimed.

Brian looked down at the foot of Mount Norumbega. On the lawns below, where once woods had stood, now billowed the nests of the Thusser. In the distance he could see the white steeples of Gerenford overgrown with Thusser warts. The Horde had spread far into the countryside.

He turned to look at Gwynyfer. She was crouched, looking upward anxiously. "What *is* it?" she said. "It's so *empty.*"

Gregory and Brian looked up. Gregory explained, "The sky. It's a sky. We have one here."

They didn't have time to explain. The giants began to speak, one word from each of them at a time. "The." — "Rules." — "Keepers." — "Have." — "Adjudicated." — "They." — "Have." — "Determined." — "A." — "Foul." — "On." — "The." — "Thusser." — "Side." — "The." — "Thusser." — "Horde." — "Have." — "Illegally." — "Occupied." — "Disputed." — "Territory." — "They." — "Shall." — "Be." — "Flushed." — "Out."

Gregory cheered and slapped Brian on the back. Brian, catching on, cheered, too.

"The." — "Thusser." — "Horde." — "Have." — "Forfeited." — "The." — "Game."

It was won. The Thusser were out.

"The." — "Rules." — "Keepers." — "Arrive."

There was a hiss, and on three sides of the gothic capsule, circular windows opened, and a great gale blew out, as if something massive had swept into the world and hovered above them.

The kids could see nothing, but they could feel the three great motions of wind. Stone bugles on the capsule blew siren-blasts of warning.

Far down in the Thusser suburbs and the deadened streets of town, other capsules appeared. Other round hatches opened. There was a noise of great winds.

Now the three invisible beings, the Rules Keepers, swept down over the slopes of Mount Norumbega. Brian and Gregory and Gwynyfer could see the treetops boil as the great presences passed — and for brief instants, they

258

got a glimpse of unearthly beings, of too many dimensions to see at once, just a quick vision of hide, a few angled limbs, many eyes. And then unseen creatures reached the Thusser subdivision and started to pull the place apart.

They blew at the great, billowing sheets of Thusser nests. They scrambled lawn furniture. They tore at houses. They dragged apart walls. And there were many of them now, all seen only through their deeds: roofs pulled asunder and fantastical walls blown apart.

Down in that suburb, Thusser fathers ran out of their houses, screaming at the Rules Keepers, preparing spells; mothers chanted magic words of ill intent; Horde children longed for something to scratch at and kill. As fast as they poured out of their houses, they were whipped away into exile, sent back to their world, draining into nothing like people made of sand.

The Thusser army, slipping though the valleys of Vermont, heard the distant blast of stone trumpets. They heard the rumble of something like a steam train rolling straight toward them through the sky. They looked up, and the few who'd trained to see other dimensions caught a glimpse of limbs and mouths and all the eyes.

The Rules Keepers fell on the Thusser army and tore it apart. Infantry in their long, black coats were hurled back into their world. Commanders struggled to keep ranks neat, but they were pulled out of their machines and spun until gone. Tanks were wrenched into pieces.

Deep below the mountain, in the City of Gargoyles, where old stone houses were cankered with blobby condos, fierce gusts slammed along the streets, pulling up Thusser

259

construction by its roots. The winds roared through the caverns. Thusser struggled against it. They cast up quick enchantments, but nothing could protect them. The Rules Keepers seized them, and their earthly bodies crumbled. Their bladder homes melted.

Slumbering bodies were left in the alleys — humans, hypnotized, who had hung in the web of Thusser settlement. They were coated with strands of insulation. They did not move. They stared, unaware, into the darkness.

Struggling over boulders and between spruce, Brian, Gregory, and Gwynyfer watched the landscape tear itself apart. They saw houses heaving. They winced as Thusser were tossed up into the air and atomized.

There was a never-ending sound of wind in their ears.

✳   ✳   ✳

In the Great Body, capsules appeared in Pflundt, and the Horde soldiers remaining there were helpless against the blasts of wind that shot down from the cliffs. They were all guilty of fouls. They had all passed illegally through the contested territory on Earth. They were all doomed to exile back in their own world.

Far out in the marshes, a capsule appeared and blew notes of warning from its stone bugles. Hatches opened. The surface of slime rippled as invisible beings shot out across it.

In small villages seized by the Horde, lean-tos and huts collapsed as the wind hit and frenzied soldiers were snatched and blinked out of being.

In the flux stream, Thusser on subs looked out into the green darkness and saw frothing, bubbling forms shoot toward them. They felt their vessels shudder. Then the things had passed through the walls and were on board with them.

Panicked soldiers clambered through hatches, pushing their mates out of the way, shoving other Thusser with knees and with hands in the face. Captains called for regimental wizards to do something — *do something* — but no one knew what they were up against. They watched their sailors disappear like monuments of sand blown by a fierce desert wind.

Subs drifted, empty, in the tide.

✳ ✳ ✳

Green waters washed through the rubble that was once New Norumbega. Hundreds of people — live and mechanical — sat on islands, watching plastic garbage drift past. Occasionally, another shudder would run through the Great Body, and everything would jump up and down. The army was drenched.

The Empress of the Innards, her gloomy Prime Minister, and Kalgrash the troll sat on a pile of fallen pillars with their elbows on their knees.

They saw a woman sloshing toward them in Wellington boots. "Your Highness!" the woman called. "Message from General Malark."

"Is he officially a general?" the Empress wondered. "I can't now recall."

The troll growled, "He's a general."

"Must you be so sour?"

The messenger started climbing the pillars. "The Thusser have stopped drilling, ma'am!" she said. "Their subs are just sitting there. Admiral Brunt is going to move in and see what the situation is."

Kalgrash perked up. "They're gone!" he said. "Gregory and Bri did it! The Thusser are gone!"

The messenger said, "General Malark says that if the navy can seize the drill ships, he'll order them to be backed slowly out of the holes they've dug. He says that the pressure of the flesh will close up the holes, as long as they're slow about it and careful with the drills."

Kalgrash stood up. He threw his arms wide. "We're saved, saved, saved!"

The Empress Elspeth inspected the messenger. "That's ripping news. We've got to send out scouts to see what's still standing. Pray where did you find those ducky Wellies?"

✳ ✳ ✳

Hopping down the side of Mount Norumbega, Gregory, Gwynyfer, and Brian felt time itself righted. The Thusser had built a bubble where seconds flowed faster — and now that bubble was tapped, and burst, and a shock wave of missing hours and crunched days slammed into the forest, the mountain, and Rumbling Elk Haven itself.

It hit the kids. Their hair flew, mussed by passing minutes.

They stumbled and fell. Their stomachs churned. Gregory retched. They saw streaks of light flash against the sky. Again, they caught quick, jolting visions of the Rules Keepers sweeping incomprehensibly through the air.

✳ ✳ ✳

Deep in the caverns beneath the mountain, one last Norumbegan, Wee Sniggleping, stirred in the darkness. He had been captured by Thusser and hung up in some settler's basement near a two-in-one washer/dryer. He looked around dully and found himself freed. He coughed and inspected his hands. Slowly, he awakened from his Thusser dreams.

He crawled along the cobbled street. Streamers of Horde nest trailed behind him. His head was pounding.

"Prudence?" he croaked. "Prudence, my dear, if you're lying on a side street near here, do give a holler. Truly: If you'll only say you're alive, my dear, I'll whip you up an omelet."

✳ ✳ ✳

The air was still. The sky was serene and blue.

At the foot of Mount Norumbega, nothing moved. The landscape was one gigantic jumble. There were vast red scrapes of wet earth where nothing grew. The suburban houses of humans lay in crumpled piles: wallboard, clapboard, sheets of shingles; struts and frames and marble countertops. Plaster dust and two-by-fours. Sleeping owners were curled among the ruins. Streets were cracked. Cars were overturned.

For miles, nothing was whole.

A thin blond boy, a stocky boy with dark hair and glasses, and an elfin girl from another world stood and surveyed the wreckage.

They did not speak in their astonishment.

TWENTY-SEVEN

The next day, the Imperial Council of New Norumbega, rulers of all the Empire of the Innards, gathered on a hilltop to greet the Umpire officially. Their clothes were torn and muddy. Their faces were proud and weary. Their city was huge mound of garbage surrounded by a vast lake of green.

The lux effluvium burned pitilessly in the sky above them. The lake steamed in the heat.

The Empress sat upon her throne. Someone had found a swivel chair and covered it with a blue sheet. Girls stood holding a canopy over her. To either side of her stood Kalgrash and General Malark, holding huge ceremonial axes. The Court stood on rubble, all in a large circle.

The Umpire Capsule appeared in the midst of them all, the chapel carried by its three mechanical giants. It blinked into being. The door opened, and three kids stepped out, accompanied by a small, lively, and curious bacterium.

Gwynyfer Gwarnmore saw her father, the duke, and hobbled toward him.

"Why, hullo, old thing," said the duke, putting his arms around her. "Living and breathing?"

"Only just."

"We've had a frightful time of it since you've been gone."

The Empress roared, "Is there no decorum?"

Gwynyfer Gwarnmore bowed painfully before her ruler. She spoke the formal greeting. She introduced Brian and Gregory as if they'd never been at court before. She said nothing about Tars the friendly germ.

Then there was a *whoosh*, and one of the Rules Keepers was among them. It could not be seen, except perhaps by the Court's wizards. Everyone could feel it towering over them however.

The Earl of Munderplast stepped forward in his muddy robes and bowed to the empty air. He declared, "The Court of Her Sublime Highness Elspeth, the Empress of Old Norumbega, New Norumbega, and the Whole Dominion of the Innards, Electoress of the Bladders, Queen of the Gastric Wastes, Sovereign of Ducts Superior and Inferior WELCOMES the Rules Keepers established by ancient custom in the Treaty of Pellerine, and we delight that they enter our Empress's divine and fearsome presence."

The three mechanical guardians of the capsule turned their heads toward the Empress Elspeth.

"The." — "Rules." — "Keepers." — "Greet." — "The." — "Empress." — "Of." — "Norumbega."

She nodded.

"The." — "Rules." — "Keepers." — "Have." — "Determined." — "That." — "The." — "Thusser." — "Horde." — "Were." — "In." — "Violation." — "Of." — "The." — "Agreed." — "Terms." — "Of." — "The." — "Contest." There was a pause. "Accordingly." — "The." — "Thusser." — "Are." — "Banished."

There was a ragged cheer. The Council was relieved.

The Empress said, "Old Norumbega is ours again? The whole kingdom under the mountain?"

"Old." — "Norumbega." — "Is." — "Yours." — "In." — "Title." — "Full." — "And." — "Clear."

"Well, that is just delightful. Things had gotten a little grimmers around here."

General Malark stepped forward and bowed first at the Empress, then at the unseen Rules Keeper. "Your Highness," he said, "the Mannequin Army shall make immediate preparations for the evacuation of the Great Body. With the submarines we have seized, we will start to shuttle civilians down to Three-Gut and to the portal between the worlds. We should be able to empty the Great Body of both breathing and mechanical Norumbegans within two weeks."

Brian's heart swelled with joy. The mannequins were going to make it out of the Great Body. And their one-time masters, too. The City of Gargoyles, empty for centuries, would be full of people. Everyone was going to be safe. They wouldn't have to trust this strange, mammoth creature in which blood-tides were changing. The landscape was rumbling and at any moment, thousands of miles could be swamped in goo.

He and the others had done a good job, he realized. They had stuck with their mission, in spite of everything — all of them working together. It was over. Things could get back to how they were before the Thusser invaded the old country, four hundred long years earlier.

Brian smiled at Gregory and Gwynyfer. Victory was sweet.

Lord Attleborough-Stoughton was the first to step forward in protest. "Your Highness," said his lordship, sweeping his dusty top hat off his head. "We cannot possibly leave the Great Body. We have built an empire here. It would be" — he paused briefly to think — "It would be unpatriotic."

Duke Gwarnmore was the next to speak up. "Attleborough-Stoughton is right, ma'am. We can't possibly leave. Anyone who suggests crawling back to that hole under the mountain is a defeatist."

"Probably a traitor," said Attleborough-Stoughton. "A thin-blooded traitor and a fool. No true Norumbegan."

Duke Gwarnmore said, "If the bally manns are suggesting we do a thing, why the deuce should we do it? They're nothing but windup upstarts. Rebels."

Brian goggled. They were saying these things, he could tell, just because they didn't want to lose their position and their land. He burbled, "Don't listen to them!" And to the men themselves: "You're just — both of you — you just don't want to give up your railroads! And your estates! But no one can stay here! You can't!"

"The baboon's right," said the Empress Elspeth. "We can't stay here. Who knows when this awful body will get up on its haunches and suddenly up will be down and we'll all be washed to kingdom come."

"We don't know it has haunches," said Duke Gwarnmore. "We don't know that it has any limbs at all. We could be perfectly safe."

There was a murmur of "Mm, yes," among the courtiers. They all had property they wanted to protect. And it was beneath them to evacuate, like a bunch of superstitious peasants in head scarves. None of them wanted to abandon their domains and their plantations and their fortresses in the kinks of ducts.

"No one can make us do a thing," said the Duchess Gwarnmore. "We are Norumbegans."

Brian said, *"You can't — you can't just endanger everyone in the empire, all your subjects, just so you can keep ahold of some stupid spleen or something! And the railroads! All of you? This is crazy!"*

He wouldn't have been able to speak that way to adults, just a few weeks earlier. But he could tell that in this case, it wasn't a bad thing to shout.

The Empress seemed to agree with him. "It does seem a little shabby to squat here, chaps, when there's a whole castle and some first-rate boulevards waiting for us back in the old home." She squinted into the distance. "Attleborough-Stoughton," she said, "your railroads are under this noisome swamp. That's a thing that requires a thorough thinking-over."

269

This didn't worry his lordship. "Subaquatic railroad cars!" Attleborough-Stoughton exclaimed. "If we can't drain the lake."

"Lakefront property," said Duke Gwarnmore. "We all of us own a great deal of it, now."

"Lakefront property!" agreed his wife. "He's not wrong about that! I see resorts! Grand hotels! Water-skiing! Paddle boats! Women in white with parasols estivating in the ventricles!"

"Yes," cried Lord Attleborough-Stoughton, "on the shores of Lake Elspeth."

Now the Empress looked interested. "What was that?" she said. "It could be called Lake Elspeth?"

"Of course, Your Sublime Highness," said Duke Gwarnmore, bowing.

Brian was hysterical with anger. *"What are you talking about?"* he cried. *"You're all going to die! You're going to be digested or ... or ... or smooshed .... or ..."*

"Tell the little mite to clamp his mouth shut," said the Empress, "or we're dunking him in Lake Elspeth."

The courtiers clapped at their sovereign's wit.

"Why," she said, smiling out over her dominion, "it seems, lads and ladies, that the old Dry Heart ain't quite so dry no more!"

✳ ✳ ✳

It was time for the capsule to go. It was going back to Earth, where it would be forever deactivated.

Brian and Gregory were going back with it. Tars the joyous germ could tell something was happening, so he stuck by Brian's side. He wanted to go wherever Brian was going.

Gwynyfer Gwarnmore, of course, would not even think about going back to Earth.

Brian was not sorry to see the last of her. He shook her hand and watched Gregory and Gwynyfer walk off, their hands touching.

Brian turned to Kalgrash. "You sure you don't want a ride back?"

"Naw," said Kalgrash. "Even though most of the breathers are staying — crazy, crazy, crazy — the mannequins are going to evacuate, and I'm going to help. We're gone. We're going to try to save whatever Norumbegans want to give up this dump and come with us. The general and I are going to organize the evacuation."

"That's really nice of you. You're so great. But you don't know how long the Great Body is going to be safe," said Brian. "What if in two weeks it's all the way back alive, and everything's moving around and flushing and pumping brunch all over the place and stuff?"

Kalgrash promised him, "Two weeks, and we'll be eating Fudgsicles at the top of Norumbega Mountain." He crossed his mechanical heart.

"Okay," said Brian. "All right."

He had that strange feeling in his gut that everything was over. The adventure was done. Time to go home.

Not too far away, Gregory stood with Gwynyfer on a

concrete heap. He put his arms around her. It felt good to hold on to her. He said, "I can't believe you're staying. I'm going to . . ." He couldn't talk. He didn't want her to hear that he was crying. He pressed his chin into her shoulder and wiped his eyes.

"You've been terrific fun," said Gwynyfer. "We did things I never would have done."

"I'll never forget it," said Gregory. He waited, but she wasn't saying anything, so he hinted, "What about you, Gwynyfer? Will you ever forget all of this?"

She patted his back kindly. "No, of course not, Human G."

"Norumbegan G," he whispered. He held on to her as hard as he could.

And then he realized she was waiting for him to stop. She was looking over his shoulder. She was silent because she was watching friends of hers skipping around in the green water. Boys in shorts kicking up spray. She was smiling. She was anxious to get down to the water's edge.

He let go of her. He almost pushed her away.

She smiled wistfully at him. She touched his face. "Bye, then," she said.

"Yeah," he mumbled. "Bye."

Ski trips crumpled and slid down slopes. So did school dances, him and Gwyn arm in arm, and eating at restaurants, and pulling each other along the streets of New York, and sitting on mountaintops in New Hampshire. All of it balled up and hurled downhill and it didn't matter anymore anyway.

He walked to the capsule. When he turned back to look at her, she was already bounding down the trash heap on her bad leg, calling out to old friends.

Gregory stepped into the open door. Brian was already there with Tars, waiting to be transported.

The Empress of the Innards walked through the mounds, the girls holding the canopy above her. In their torn tails and punched-in derbies, the Court followed behind her, giggling at her jokes.

This was the last glimpse Brian and Gregory ever had of the Court of Norumbega.

✳ ✳ ✳

Two weeks later, a final caravan of mechanical refugees made its way across the ooze of Three-Gut. Everything was in turmoil. Wind howled. The air was filled with flying sludge. Slow waves of goop smashed across the prows of the sleds, almost rolling over the thombulants that dragged them. Through the veins in the sky, jolts of electric light jittered through the lux effluvium.

It was not clear whether the Great Body was ever going to quiet down again. Every few hours, there were convulsions. Some geologists said that it was going to return to full life as no one had seen in living memory; some theologians said that with the Thusser gone, it would pass back into its deathly sleep. Philosophers said that everything would always be the same; poets said that the Great Body was one of a flock, all migrating

273

through some vast space, and that the flock had just spotted its goal. The noblemen and noblewomen of the Court, who did not want to leave, paid for scientific proof that everything would settle down and be just fine. That was the story that was printed in the *Norumbega Vassal-Tribune*.

Word had gone out across the Empire of the Innards that anyone who wanted to abandon the Great Body should make his or her way toward Three-Gut. Pioneer families in distant valves had given up their cabins and set out; people whose homes had been crushed in the collapse of New Norumbega decided they had nothing to lose. A few mannequins had said they would stay behind to help the breathers build again, if the violent spasms of the Great Body ever let up. Most of the mannequins, though, were traveling to a new home. They had earned it. They had received official permission for their own state before the fight with the Thusser had begun. The army had shuttled them through the heaving guts to the gateway between worlds.

In an unbuilt city in the middle of the endless sputum sea of Three-Gut, barely visible in the howling murk, Kalgrash stood on top of a flight of stairs. Beside him shimmered the portal to Earth. In two weeks, a few thousand mannequins and a few hundred breathers had passed through to find a new life in old haunts.

Now the last load of passengers was there. They wobbled down the gangplanks from their sleds. Their drivers cut loose the thombulants. They let them roam.

Thombulants would do better than mannequins or elves if the Body came to full life.

The pilgrims toiled up the steps with globs of splutter smacking on their coats. It was thick as cookie dough. They shielded their glass eyes with hoods.

"These the last?" the troll shouted to Dantzig, the pilot.

Dantzig nodded.

"Step on through!" said the troll over the gale. Blue light from above sparked and flared. His armor shone. "We're done, done, done!" He cackled in joy.

The mechanical pilgrims stepped through the portal. Kalgrash and Dantzig followed.

Suddenly, everything was silent. There was no storm. There was no giant Body heaving. It was dark and quiet and warm.

They were in a little tomb, and General Malark sat at a card table, checking their names off a list. They were beneath the mountains of Vermont.

"That it?" said the troll.

Malark nodded fiercely. "That's it," he said.

Kalgrash sighed. He was back on Earth.

"Okay," said Malark. "Let's close the gate."

Wizards moved to either side of the portal. They touched runes. They spoke things. It did not take long. Kalgrash watched, while around him, the pilgrims muttered in the catacombs.

With a flutter of air, the gate between the worlds was closed forever.

"So there," whispered Kalgrash.

Back in Three-Gut, the portal to Earth was suddenly not a space, but a slab. It stood on the top of a staircase to nowhere. The storm raged around it. No one would ever pass through it again.

In the distance, thombulants, pudgy and free, romped in muck.

EPILOGUE

"**A** tempest touches down in a small Vermont town" was how the news told the story, and they spoke of cyclones and force-four tornadoes. Men in ties argued about how such destruction could fall out of clear skies. The wind was to blame, and had torn apart two hundred houses. Worse, in the weeks that followed, the government announced that the twister had burst tanks at a local chemical plant, releasing some kind of gas, some neurotoxin that caused hallucinations and loss of memory in victims throughout the area.

There was, in reality, no chemical plant, no neurotoxin, no invisible gas — but there was also no explanation for all the people who struggled out of the wreckage, half starved, with vague memories of demons dancing in the suburb streets. There was no reason that several hundred people should have no memory of weeks just passed, or should lie in a stupor until awoken. It was better to have an excuse. Someone typed one and printed out copies.

So the news talked about chemicals blown through the air, and there were shots of ruined houses. There were clips of Red Cross volunteers in sagging mesh vests reaching out their hands to pull people out of the debris. There were pictures of wide streets flanked on both sides by ruined mounds of planking, and a family in the middle of the street, clutching one another against the ruddy sky. There was a helicopter shot of kids who were found dazed at an intersection, riding their bikes in a circle counterclockwise, as if aping the rotation of the twister.

The human victims of the Thusser invasion spent weeks in the hospital. They were told of poisonous gas, but among themselves, they whispered about a curse. They knew something evil had stalked their streets. Many of them never went back to the ruins of Rumbling Elk Haven to claim the things that had not been destroyed.

No word ever came from the Great Body as to whether the Empire of the Innards survived the new convulsions or not. Perhaps the body settled down, and the Imperial Court still dances in lines as it once did. Perhaps, as seems more likely, the Great Body revived and even moved, shaking apart a whole civilization in moments, drowning them in its own weird fluids. Perhaps, in the midst of cataclysm and devastation, they regretted their decision to stay. Regardless, they made their choice, and they have never been heard from again.

The Norumbegan breathers who'd returned to Earth quickly disappeared. Some went to live in remote caverns of the old underground kingdom. Most of them set off to Europe to find their ancient cousins and to see the hidden cities that their ancestors had left more than two thousand years before.

The mannequins inherited the City of Gargoyles. They told themselves that they were keeping it ready for the return of their old masters — but they knew that their masters would never return. They had been promised their freedom if they beat the Thusser, and now, in the ancient city where they had been built to serve generations before, they declared a Republic of Automatons, a commonwealth of mannequins. The subterranean city came to life again. They even lit the sun.

One day a couple of months after the Rules Keepers swept the Game board clean, Brian and Gregory and Kalgrash sat on the side of Mount Norumbega with Wee Sniggleping and Gregory's cousin Prudence, who'd awakened from her Thusser slumber with the rest. It was getting cold already. The fall had come. The humans wore coats. Tars the heraldic bacterium was curled around Brian like a couple of belts.

Wee Sniggleping ate an apple. He chewed while he talked. He explained that he was training the mannequins to remove their loyalty to the old Norumbegans. It had to be done carefully, and with a very small screwdriver. "Important, though, that they do it before they write the constitution for their Republic. Otherwise the idiots will be calling it a Protectorate and waiting for the Empress to come back in glory and sit on their shoulders."

Brian asked him, "What'll you do, now that the Game is over?"

"Backgammon. I've been teaching the troll. Once he stopped eating the pieces, he was a quick study."

Kalgrash lifted up his mighty arm and watched himself flex his mailed hand. "I've been thinking, now that we have some free time, I should go back to having the smaller body. And naked. Whadaya think? I don't think there's going to be as much smiting. And I like to eat in the buff. Helps digestion."

"Interesting," said Prudence, leaning back on her elbows.

Gregory asked, "What about you, Prudence?"

"I wear clothes at mealtimes."

"No. What are you going to do?"

She made a noise. "I wonder if I can move back into my house. It's been condemned because of the 'chemical plant explosion.'" She rolled her eyes.

Brian looked down over the mess below them: the empty fields of mud, the torn-up houses, the toppled trees. He said, "Why didn't the Rules Keepers put everything back the way it was before the Thusser broke the Rules? I wish they could put the forest back. It was huge. It was so old. I can't believe it was all pulled up."

"Gone, gone, gone," said Kalgrash sadly.

They looked down at what remained of the fir forest on the slopes, the maples beginning to turn beside old stone walls. The few wrecked oaks between the cellar holes of suburbs.

Staring down at all of it, Snig hefted his apple and hurled it. He said, "That's right, Mr. Thatz. What's gone is gone. But in twenty years, there'll be a little forest there again. You'll be here. You'll see it. And when you're sixty, when you're seventy, you'll climb the mountain, and the trees down there will be tall. Tall enough to get lost in. Tall enough for paths and clearings. You'll look at the forest, and you'll remember right now, us sitting here, me talking. And a hundred and fifty years from now, the woods will be old, and they'll look like they did the day you first came here. Just like when you and Gregory drove up a year ago in that carriage. You'll be dead by then, of course. You'll be gone. But the forest will look like it did when you were just a boy. And under the mountain, they'll still be telling stories about you. The machines will tell the tale of you and Gregory and Prudence and the Game. Kalgrash and I will still be alive, I suppose. We'll tell the story."

Brian said suddenly, "I want to live here. I want to live near you all." He looked desperately at them. He knew that's what he would do. Somehow, as soon as possible.

He realized as he said this that he was saying it to Prudence and Kalgrash and Wee Snig — that he hadn't looked at Gregory. He hadn't thought about Gregory and where he might end up. Guiltily, he turned to his friend.

Gregory hadn't noticed. The boy was looking out over the mountains, thinking thoughts he didn't say.

Brian would be back as often as possible. He wanted to see the Mannequin Republic thrive. He wanted to ice skate with Kalgrash in the winter. He wanted to be able to keep Tars the heraldic bacterium as a pet without hiding the poor germ in a duffel bag or on the top shelf of his closet. It didn't matter what happened: He would be here.

281

There they sat on Mount Norumbega. It was a republic of brave and hopeful mannequins. Four hundred years before that, it had been an empire, old and lazy. A thousand years earlier, by the reckoning of humans, it had been a young kingdom. Before that, it had just been a mountain where hunters came to find wolves. Fir and spruce grew on the heights. There were silver swamps on its belly, surrounded by birch. Porcupines found hollows in the moss. Glaciers had scraped across it in unimaginable aeons of frost. Once it had been under a sea.

Now, for a little time one day, these six sat upon its slopes. They ate apples.

The wind blew from the south.